A Place to Belong

AN OPPOSITES ATTRACT ROMANCE

ALEXA RIVERS

A Place to Belong
Copyright © 2021 by Alexa Rivers
All rights reserved.
All rights reserved worldwide.

Cover Design © Designed with Grace
Formatting: Indie Pen PR
Editing: Essential Edits
Proofreading: Yvette Deon
Beta Reader: Meredith Sigrist
Managed by: Indie Pen PR

Print ISBN number: 978-0-9951492-3-6

 Created with Vellum

From Alexa Rivers comes an opposites attract romance packed with humor, emotion and a sizzling happily ever after.

Horror author Felicity Bell moves to the charming town of Oak Bend after being shunned from the last place she called home. When she walks in the door of her new rental, she doesn't expect to find a half-naked man standing in her kitchen. There's just one problem: Wyatt Dawson seems to think it's *his* kitchen. Misunderstandings aside, her new neighbor is lumberjack hot, and his grumpiness only makes her more determined to bring a little joy to his life, even if he'd rather be left alone.

Burned by his past, Wyatt isn't about to let the cheerful free spirit next door into his heart only for her to crush him when she flits out of town again. But with his well-meaning, matchmaking, mother on the case, these two end up spending far too much time together and things between the unlikely pair quickly heat up. It may be true what they say—opposites do attract, but only if their relationship can survive Wyatt's interfering ex-girlfriend and Felicity's fear of history repeating itself.

Welcome to Oak Bend, where blue-collar hotties work hard and love even harder, especially when it comes to landing their happily ever after.

To Michelle and Judy –
Thanks for helping me create Wyatt Dawson.

CHAPTER 1

FELICITY

I PARK my car outside a tidy house with cream-painted boards and a neatly kept garden, and I nod in approval. Yes, this could be home. Not a bad effort for something I found in a half-hour Google search before packing my things into the trunk of my Ford Focus and driving out of Clearwater, never to return. Okay, so maybe I'm a little dramatic, but anyone who's been rejected as many times as I have generally is. The truth is, I've turned moving on into an art form. Hence my new rental—a charming turn-of-the-century building set amongst similar homes on a quiet street in the Michigan town of Oak Bend.

Leaning back in my seat, I study the place through the car window. It has dusky blue windowsills, a few flowers in the front garden, and an old-fashioned porch with a seat where I'll be able to watch the world go by. Or at least the two cars per hour that probably average along this stretch of road. I grab the keys my landlady, Nadine, gave me and get out, then collect one of my suitcases and lock up behind me. Experience has taught me that even in cute towns like this one, bad things can happen. Clutching the keys tighter, I wander up the cracked concrete path that leads around the side of the property. Nadine told me to enter through the back, and when I climb the two steps to the door and try the handle, it's unlocked. Hesitantly, I push it further open and peer inside. I don't see anything, but I can smell coffee, which is strange. The rental is supposed to be empty. I waver on the doorstep. Should I go in and investigate or back off and call her?

I step inside. While I may not look like much, it takes more than a mug of coffee to scare me. Perhaps Nadine sent someone around to clean up before I arrived. As I place my suitcase on the kitchen floor and look around, I notice there's enough clutter to give the appearance of someone living here. A stack of unwashed dishes lie in the sink. A bowl of fruit sits on the end of the counter. The distinct aroma of cooked chicken hangs in the air. Does Nadine's house have a squatter?

Elsewhere, I hear a shower turn off. I hadn't even noticed the sound of running water until suddenly it was gone. Clasping the keys in my fist, I slot one between my fingers like I was taught in self-defense class. *Eyes, then groin.* I tense, waiting for the squatter to emerge. Steam billows into the doorway opposite me, which leads deeper into the house, and a man appears within it.

What a man.

My jaw drops, my stomach riots, and a fizzle of something hot shoots down my spine. I lick my lips. Nadine's squatter is hands-down the hottest half-naked male I've ever had the privilege of shrieking at.

Because I *do* shriek.

It's the loudest, shrillest, most repulsive noise I've ever made in my life—and trust me, that's saying something. I'm not quiet by nature. He flinches, his gaze shooting over to me, and the movement shakes the towel around his waist loose. Next thing I know, I'm staring at six-feet-two-inches of bare, sexy man. I can't tear my eyes away. I should use my brain and put some distance between us, but instead my gaze skates down a muscular chest dusted with dark hair, pausing to admire arms like twin pythons, then drops to the snake between his legs.

Holy crap.

He's perfection. Thick and long, but not cumbersome, with a little hair. As I gawk, his body seems to ripple as though it likes my attention—although God knows why. I'm a stranger. A shrieking stranger. And he's a weird, naked squatter. Clapping a hand to my eyes, I stop myself from continuing the visual exploration down his meaty thighs. But then I remove my hand as I realize I don't know what his intentions toward me are. Is he harmless? He doesn't look harmless.

"What are you doing in my house?" I demand.

He bends and reaches for the towel, then cinches it around his waist before meeting my eyes. His lips part, and a breath gusts between them. It's the first time I've paid much attention to his face, which is a work of art. Eyes the color of melted chocolate, a straight nose, and a strong jaw that's partially hidden by a close-trimmed beard. It's his eyes that hit me hardest. Their intensity sends a disturbing array of thoughts through my mind—thoughts of seeing them darken with passion while I investigate everything he's hiding behind that towel.

Get your mind out of the gutter.

"Your house?" he asks, his voice hardly more than a rumble I can feel to my bones. "Last I checked, I'm the one who pays the bills, so I'm the one who asks the questions. Who are you, and how did you get in?"

Wringing my hands, the flutters in my gut morph from attraction to anxiety. Whatever is going on here, I don't like it. This man is getting in the way of my plans for the evening—namely, to settle into my new home and track down a local eatery. I'm not a person who handles conflict well, and it seems we might have a big disagreement on our hands if we both think we have a claim over this house.

"I rented it this morning," I explain, my words spilling out one on top of the other, as they tend to do when I get nervous. "I signed a rental agreement and everything. I'm sure there must be a mistake. Have you signed an agreement?"

"No," he replies, one hand going to his hip. "I don't need to, because my name is on the deed."

"Oh." I swallow. What on earth is going on here? He takes a step toward me, and I throw one hand up as if to ward him off. "Please stay there."

I don't want this guy anywhere near me. He might be deranged. Even if he's sane, his state of undress is too alarming for my peace of mind.

He scowls. "We can get to the bottom of this if you let me get the deed from my safe. But first, I need the key, which is in the kitchen drawer."

"Wait, wait, wait." How do I know he isn't just going to attack me when he gets close? "There's no need for that. I'll go without a fuss as soon as I've called my landlady to clear this up."

I reach for my phone with the hand that isn't warding him off, and the keys jangle. His gaze fixes on them, and then he drags a palm down his face and groans.

"Don't bother calling. I know what's going on."

Wyatt

I SHOULD HAVE KNOWN the moment I saw her that this was no coincidence. A hot crazy lady randomly appears in my house? Not fucking likely. This has Mom's fingerprints all over it, and the keys clutched in the blonde's hand are the nail in her coffin. I sigh. The woman is eyeing me like I'm a rabid dog about to strike. Or at least, that's how she's looking at me *now*. I caught the flash of heat in her gaze when my towel dropped a moment ago.

Groaning again, I lean against the doorframe and wonder what I did to deserve this. I've spent a long day completing work on a brick fence. My back aches, and all I want is to crack open a beer and watch hockey.

"So?" The blonde clasps her hands together, fidgeting. She's pretty, if a bit skittish. Her moss-green eyes dart around the kitchen, returning to me every few seconds as though she's wary of taking her attention off me for too long. "What's going on?"

I nod toward the keys in her hand. "Those belong to my mother. She owns the house next door, which is the one you actually rented."

"Oh." Her slim shoulders slump in relief, and her curls bounce. "Thank goodness for that. It's all a big misunder-standing."

I laugh dryly. "It's no such thing."

A furrow forms between her brows. "What do you mean? Surely she just gave me the wrong set of keys."

"If only."

She seems baffled by my cryptic comment, and I sigh, already able to tell that she's the type who's curious enough to stick around until I explain everything.

"Mom intentionally sent you here," I say, figuring I may

as well get the awkwardness out of the way. I'm sure it's not the only time she'll be subject to Mom's match-making machinations if she plans to live next door. She has a wholesome, sweet vibe that Mom will just eat up.

Yeah, I'm going to be dodging this woman for the foreseeable future.

"She hoped we'd run into each other, and that I'd be smitten with you. She set us up."

"*Oh.*" This time, there's a whole other level of meaning to the word. But then she cocks her head, and the furrow deepens. "I wouldn't have thought you needed to be set up." Her gaze rakes over me once again, and I can't help but puff out my chest. It's been a long time since anyone looked at me with such blatant appreciation, and I can tell she doesn't even realize she's doing it, or else she'd be mortified.

"I don't," I reply firmly, and her eyes snap up to mine. A delicate, pink flush journeys down her neck. Damn, I need to get rid of her before I actually do start to find her charming. "Here. I'll get you my key for the place next door, and you can give me that one." I nod at the key in her hand. She drops it on the counter.

"I'm so sorry about this." She wrings her hands, looking awkward as fuck. "I didn't mean to just walk into your house and make myself at home."

"I know you didn't," I assure her. "I'm going to come closer now, is that okay?"

She nods, but her eyes remain on me as I enter the kitchen and head for the key hook by the fridge. I remove the one for the rental and replace it with the key she left on the counter, then offer her the one she actually needs. Our fingers brush as she takes it, and something jolts in my chest. Shaking it off, I snatch my hand away and check that the towel is still secure. The last thing I need is to give her another peep show.

"That key will open the front door of the house next door. Hold onto it for now, and I'll get Mom to drop by with the proper key tomorrow."

"I can do that." She smiles, and I resist the urge to fall back a step, because it lights up her entire face, elevating her from pretty to gut-wrenchingly beautiful. "I don't want to put you out any more than you already are."

"Don't worry about it." Despite my frustration, I find my lips curving. "It's not you I'm angry at."

Her expression softens. "Please don't be too mad with Nadine. She seems like such a nice person, and I'm sure she only wants to make you happy."

Damn, she has a point. But whether her intentions are good or not, it's not going to stop me from giving Mom a piece of my mind. She needs to know it's not all right to hand out my house key to total strangers just because she wants grandbabies.

"Hey." Her smile diminishes. "I just realized—I didn't get your name."

"Wyatt."

"I'm Felicity. It's lovely to meet you." She offers a hand, and I look meaningfully down at the towel. I'd rather hold onto it if possible. She drops her hand, giggling. "Oops, forgot about that." She hefts her suitcase—a faded blue thing —off the ground. "Maybe I'll see you tomorrow?"

"I'm not much of a people person."

Her smile vanishes, and I feel an unwelcome pang of regret. It's better for her to find out now that I'm an unsocial prick rather than letting her get her hopes up only to have me dash them. I'm not the kind of neighbor who has barbe-cues in their back yard and invites the entire block to visit.

"Well." She tucks a strand of hair behind her ear. "Once again, I'm sorry. I'll see you when I see you."

She starts toward the door.

"Wait," I call. She stops in her tracks and glances over her shoulder. "Let me help with your bags."

For a moment, her radiant smile reappears. "Thank you, but I'm excellent at carrying my own baggage." She pauses, then turns back toward me and squares her shoulders. "Also," she takes a deep breath and releases it, "I'm a horror author." She makes the announcement as though she expects lightning to strike her down. "Is that going to be a problem?"

One of my eyebrows shoots up. I have to admit, it's a surprise. I'd never have expected the sunny little blonde to write scary stories for a living—I'd pegged her more as the kindergarten teacher type—but I don't understand why she's waiting for my response with as much dread as if she'd told me she was a leper.

I shrug. "Nope. Don't know why it would be. I'm a brick mason. You're not going to hold that against me, are you?"

"Of course not." Her shoulders relax. "Thank you, Wyatt."

"For what?" I ask, bemused, but she just shakes her head and wriggles the fingers of her free hand in a wave as she exits. Going to the window, I watch her round the corner and disappear from sight.

One thing is for sure. My new neighbor will be more interesting that the previous one.

CHAPTER 2

FELICITY

It's weird how flattered I am that Nadine likes me enough to want to set me up with her son. I mean, she went about everything the wrong way, but she clearly thought I was daughter-in-law material, even after I told her what I do for a living. The last time I came clean about my job, I was ostracized. One of my new friends took it in her head to read my novels and realized exactly how messed up my mind is. I don't blame her, but it hurt. My heart squeezes at the memory. Oh God, did it hurt. I thought I'd finally found a place to call home. I guess at least I learned a lesson from what happened. This time, I'll put my cards on the table before I get attached to anyone.

I let myself into the rental, which is similar to Wyatt's house, only without such a nice garden and minus the cushy chair on the porch. The front door opens onto a hallway, with rooms to each side. At the end of the hall, there's a lounge, and if the layout is the same as next door, I assume the kitchen is beyond that. Dragging my suitcase inside, I take stock of the place. High ceilings, textured white wallpaper, and a faint lemony scent—perhaps an air freshener. I check each of the three bedrooms and opt for the one with the large window overlooking the front garden, with a window seat tucked inside it. I've always wanted one of those to pass a summer's day reading on.

Leaving my suitcase inside, I head out to the porch, where I lower myself down and dangle my feet off the edge of the step. Grabbing my phone from the pocket of my skirt, I think about the changes I could make. Daffodils in the flowerbeds. Roses along the drive. Maybe a bird fountain in the center of the lawn if Nadine doesn't mind. I find her contact details and hit "call". Perhaps Wyatt intends to speak to her himself, but I'm not one to let others handle things for me.

"Felicity?" Nadine asks when she picks up. "How is everything? Have you started unpacking yet?"

"Everything is good," I assure her. "But there was a mix up. You gave me the wrong key. I just wanted to let you know that it's all sorted out now, and I have a key for the right place."

"So, you met my son?" She doesn't sound the least bit embarrassed or remorseful for foisting me on him.

"Yes, I did."

"And?" she prompts. "What do you think of him? He's handsome, isn't he? Very handy, too."

I sigh. Obviously, Wyatt was right, and she intentionally sent me to the wrong place.

"He seems nice," I say, not touching her second question with a ten-foot pole.

"How did he react? I hope he didn't throw you out. He can be temperamental at times."

"We talked it through." I hesitate, unsure how to phrase this next part but feeling like it needs to be said. "I'm flattered that you wanted me to meet him, but I doubt

10

he's the kind of man who needs to have women forced upon him."

She laughs. "You'd be surprised. He inherited his father's looks, and his heart is in a good place, but he's quite talented at avoiding eligible women."

Eligible women.

I giggle, then clap a hand over my mouth, ashamed of myself. Nadine means well, and I can hear her frustration. I shouldn't be amused by her word choice.

"Anyway." A subject change is in order. "Where's the best place to get dinner?"

She thinks for a moment. "Mickey's Diner on Main Street."

"Thanks so much. I'll head over there now."

"Ask for The Mickey Special," she suggests. "Best cheeseburger in town."

"Thanks." I smile. "I'll keep that in mind. Bye now."

"Bye, Felicity. Let me know if you need anything."

I hang up and finish unpacking the car, then follow GPS directions to Main Street, which is a wide, straight street lined with shops and food joints. Mickey's Diner is on a corner, and I find it easily. The place has large glass windows out the front, and when I head inside, the smell of fried food tickles my nostrils. I cross the floor to the counter, and I'm greeted by a busty woman in her fifties, with hair dyed a vivid shade of red and piled in a bun atop her head.

"Hi, hon." She leans one forearm on the counter and smiles. "You new in town?"

My cheeks heat. "Is it that obvious?"

One of her brows arches. "If you've lived here as long as I have. So, what's your story? Just passing through or staying a while?"

"Staying a while, I hope." I resist the urge to fidget when

she studies me with interest. "I've just moved into a rental on Cherry Avenue."

"Huh." She cocks her head. "Nadine Dawson's place?"

I nod, and she chuckles, the sound husky.

"She'll be pleased about that." Her sly tone says she knows exactly what tricks Nadine has already played, and I can't help but wonder if this is one of those towns where everyone knows everyone else's business. "What is it that you do, sweetheart?"

"I'm a writer." Straightening my back, I add, "I write horror novels."

Intrigue flares in her eyes. "I never met a writer before. I'm going to pick your brain about that one day, but for now, what can I get you?"

"Uh." I scan the menu written on a blackboard behind her, trying to recall what Nadine recommended. "The Mickey Special?"

She grins. "That a question or an answer?"

"Answer," I say firmly.

"Good choice." She makes no move to write my order down. "What flavor shake do you want?"

"What are my options?"

"Chocolate, caramel," she ticks them off on her fingers, "strawberry, or lime."

"Strawberry, please."

"Great. Have a seat and I'll get that out to you soon."

I sit at one of the stalls spaced along the counter, leaving the tables for people who arrive in groups. There's no use taking one up by myself. While I wait for my food, I people-watch, one of my favorite hobbies. Several of the men in the diner look like long-haul truck drivers who've stopped for a meal, and there are two young families. In one corner is a classically good-looking man in a police uniform. He's digging into a meatloaf, and when he spots me, a dimple pops in his cheek and he winks. I smile back, then glance away.

The cheeseburger, when it arrives, is as delicious as promised, and the fries are pretty good too. I finish as much as I can then sip my shake and reflect on the day. It didn't start off well, but I'm optimistic that things will improve. I have a good feeling about Oak Bend. And yeah, maybe I got off on the wrong foot with my next-door neighbor, but he seems nice enough and any tension between us is easily remedied by a plate of homemade cookies. You can never go wrong with cookies. By the time I leave, I've made up my mind that come tomorrow, Wyatt Dawson will be pleased to have me nearby.

Wyatt

ON SATURDAY MORNING, I knock on the door of the house Mom shares with my sister Julia. Mom opens it, already beaming, and I hold up the toolkit I brought with me.

"Gonna fix that leaky faucet."

"Thanks, darling." She kisses my cheek. "Come in. Jules is cooking breakfast."

I cringe. "Uh oh."

I love my sister, but the woman cannot cook to save herself.

Mom holds her hands out and shrugs. "Not much we can do when she insists on trying."

"I can hear that!" Julia calls from the kitchen. "And I'll have you know that these pancakes are going to be the best you've ever tasted."

Mom and I share a look, certain they won't be.

"Okay, Jules," I call, to placate her.

"They will," she insists, and then there's a bang and I hear her muttering to herself. I follow the sound of her voice through the living room and into the kitchen, where she's on her hands and knees cleaning something from the floor. She sits back on her heels and glares up at me. "Don't say it."

"I wasn't saying anything."

Her eyes narrow. "Don't even think it."

At this, I chuckle. "Sorry Jules, even you can't control my thoughts."

She grumbles and tucks a dark lock of hair into a messy bun. My baby sister is a nerdy control freak, and it bothers her to no end that she can't cook when it's basically chemistry. I drop the toolkit and get onto my hands and knees, then open the door of the cupboard beneath the sink. The leak is an easy fix, and I get to work, trying to ignore the sounds of Julia's cooking catastrophe above me. At one point, I smell pancakes, and my stomach grumbles loudly enough to be heard throughout the room.

"Glad you're hungry," Julia says. "I've got a heap of batter."

For once, I think she might have pulled off a miracle. But then the scent takes on an acrid hint. She's burned it. I climb out from beneath the sink and wash my hands, glancing at the sad stack of charred pancakes growing beside the skillet.

"Have you considered lowering the temperature?" I ask.

She rolls her eyes. "Never thought of that."

Five minutes later, the three of us sit at the dining table and force down her pancakes, which are gooey on the inside and burnt on the outside. Perhaps that's how a toasted marshmallow is supposed to be, but pancakes sure as hell aren't.

"Mom," I say, now that she's stuck here with me. "You've got to knock it off with the matchmaking."

Julia's gaze locks on Mom with interest. "Who's the girl?"

"Our new tenant." Mom winks at me. "Isn't she pretty?"

"Yeah," I grudgingly allow. "But—"

"She writes in your favorite genre," she interrupts, as though I never spoke.

Julia's eyebrows shoot up. "She's an author?"

"A *horror* author," Mom clarifies.

"That's so cool!" She grabs her phone from her pocket, and Mom looks ready to rap her on the knuckles, but then Julia asks, "What's her name?"

I shrug, not wanting to admit that Felicity is well and truly stuck in my head. How could I not remember the name when it fits her so well? Blonde, perky, and yes —pretty.

"Felicity Bell," Mom replies, and Julia taps on her touchscreen.

"Wow." Her thumb works while she scrolls, and my jaw tenses. "Gorgeous *and* talented." She raises her head and meets Mom's eyes. "Forget Wyatt. She's clearly more my type than his."

Mom laughs. "Last I heard, you were attracted to men."

Julia cocks her head, still staring at the screen. "Exceptions can be made."

My stomach rumbles again, and Julia sets her phone down and glares at me as though annoyed I'm not properly appreciating her efforts.

Mom turns to me. "You should at least try her books,

15

Wy. I downloaded one after I spoke to her yesterday morning, and I think you'd like it."

"I'm not interested in her."

"I'll read it," Julia offers.

Mom nods, then gives her attention back to me. "You can't let Dawn ruin you for all future relationships, honey."

"I'm not." The tips of my ears burn with embarrassment. "But the subject is closed."

Her face falls, and I feel like a bastard, but when the rest of the morning passes with no further mentions of Felicity, I can't bring myself to regret it.

I've arrived home and returned my toolkit to its spot in the garage when I hear a knock on the door. Wiping my hands on my jeans, I wander out of the garage and freeze. There, standing at my doorstep, is a woman with a mane of blonde curls. *Felicity*. She hasn't heard me, so I pause to examine her. She's wearing a pale pink skirt that reaches her knees and a darker pink cardigan, with a patterned pink headband holding her hair back. She looks like a cross between that chick from Legally Blonde and the one with the really high voice on The Big Bang Theory. And what's that she's holding?

Crossing the lawn, I clear my throat, and she pivots, a smile lighting her face.

"Wyatt, hi!"

"Hello." I lower my gaze to the plate in her hands because otherwise I'll have to admit that Mom and Julia were right. There's something angelic about her features. Sweet and open, as though she's never had a bad day in her life. The plate is almost worse. It's loaded high with home-made chocolate chip cookies, the chocolate bits still semi-melted and oozing. My mouth waters, and my stomach protests its dismal breakfast. Those cookies look fucking amazing.

"I think we got off on the wrong foot yesterday."

I drag my gaze back up. "Are you trying to bribe me into something?"

"No." Her smile fades. "I just wanted a re-do. We're going to be seeing a lot of each other, and I like to be friendly with my neighbors. What better way to start over than by bringing you cookies?" One side of her mouth lifts tentatively. "Everyone loves cookies."

"I don't," I say, right as my empty gut releases a roar and calls me a liar.

She grins. "Why don't you try one?" She selects the biggest, thickest cookie from the plate and offers it to me.

"Nope." I inhale, getting a good whiff of freshly baked perfection, and fold my arms over my chest to prevent myself from reaching for it. "I don't need your cookies if they're contingent on friendship or whatever else you have in mind." For all I know, she's in on this crazy matchmaking scheme with Mom.

"All I want is someone to show me around."

"I'm sure my mom would be happy to." My eyes wander down to the cookie she's still holding, and it smells so damn good I can nearly taste it.

"Oh." Her shoulders sag, and regret hits me like a punch in the gut. I hate seeing her deflated, but I can already tell she's one of those people who will run a mile with only the slightest encouragement. Then, she sneaks another peek. "Just try one. No conditions attached."

I shake my head. She shrugs one shoulder and bites into the morsel of deliciousness.

"Mm," she moans. "So good."

My muscles tighten. Fuck, why did she have to do that

17

right in front of me? The cookie looks so perfect I could cry. It's been ages since I had homemade cookies because Mom is on a diet, and Dawn, who used to make them for me, has been out of my life for six months, leaving me cookie-less.

"Okay," I relent. "Just one."

She passes me another cookie, and watches while my teeth sink into it. Chocolatey goodness explodes in my mouth. These are even better than Mom's. Soft and chewy, with the perfect ratio of chocolate to cookie dough. My sweet tooth is on the verge of having a mouth-gasm.

"They're good, right?" she asks.

I answer with a groan, and her smile becomes smug. I lick my fingers, and she holds up another. I reach for it, then stop short. What am I doing? I'm letting my easily-swayed stomach control my decision making.

"Better not," I say, weeping on the inside. "But thank you. That was delicious."

"I do have some positive traits." She retracts the proffered cookie and returns it to the plate. "I'm an excellent neighbor."

I can still taste the chocolate, and I gaze longingly at the remaining cookies. "I bet you're one of those neighbors who gets into everyone's business."

A flicker of something like hurt passes over her face. "Aren't they the best kind?"

"I prefer mine to stick to their side of the fence."

This time, she definitely flinches, and I feel like a dick. But I can't have her popping over here all the time, thinking we're going to be the best of friends. I have enough women in my life. I don't need another shoehorning her way in.

"Got it," she says, far too brightly, and turns on her heel to leave.

"Felicity..." I start to call after her, but when she glances over her shoulder, I fall silent, and she sighs and continues on her way. I rake a hand through my hair. Fuck, what a mess. Why can't I just behave like a normal human being and be polite?

Her cute, pink-clad ass disappears from view around the side of the rental house. Cursing again, I head inside and change into my running clothes. I jog a five-mile circuit, and when I'm done, I find a Tupperware container of cookies on my doorstep. The note on top reads "No strings attached".

"I won't eat them," I tell myself. But I totally do.

CHAPTER 3

FELICITY

"'I PREFER my neighbors to stick to their side of the fence,'" I mutter to myself as I hurry home after depositing the package of cookies on Wyatt's doorstep. When I first left his place following our conversation earlier, I wasn't feeling very charitable and considered eating them all myself, but after taking ten minutes to cool off, I remembered that he hadn't had *me* for a neighbor before. Perhaps he just needs to be taught the benefits of being friends with the person next door. Hence, the cookies. A peace offering to show that I'm genuine and don't just want to bribe him into being my tour guide. Although I do need someone to play that role.

Instead of going inside, I lock the door and redirect to my car. It takes a few minutes to drive to Nadine's house, and as I park, I notice a van up the drive that has the name of a landscaping company painted on the side. Closing my door, I scan the garden. A man clambers up from the ground and wipes his hands on his jeans. Meanwhile, I try not to drool. The guy is a hunk. Six feet of lean, chiseled muscle, with dirty blond hair and eyes a similar shade to my own.

"Well, hey there," he drawls, with a hint of a southern accent. "I didn't realize Nadine was expecting company."

"She's not." I walk toward him, and he meets me halfway. Up close, he's even more gorgeous. There's a glimmer in his eye that's all about humor and mischief. "I'm Felicity."

"Davis." He offers a hand. "The hired help."

I answer with a smile. His smirk gives me the impression he doesn't believe he's only 'the hired help' any more than I do. "Lovely to meet you, Davis."

His lips twitch, as if in amusement. "The pleasure is all mine, Felicity."

"*Davis Gentry!*"

We both swing around at the sound of Nadine's voice. She's standing atop her porch, hands on hips, watching us with interest.

"Are you flirting with my new tenant?"

"No, Ma'am," he replies, and winks at me. I giggle. I get the feeling he's a lot of fun. "Just introducing myself."

"Sure you are." She starts down the steps with a swing in her stride. "The same way you introduce yourself to anyone in a skirt. But you steer clear of Felicity. She's for Wyatt."

"Excuse me?" I squeak, my cheeks reddening.

She waves a hand dismissively. "Oh, you know what I mean."

"No, I really don't."

Davis openly chuckles. Nadine gives me an indulgent look, as if I'm playing coy. "If you say so. Anyway, what can I help you with?"

"I'm looking for someone to show me around town. Help introduce me to the locals. Would you mind?"

She frowns. "Why would you ask me when Wyatt is right next door?"

Nervously, I twist the ring on my left hand. "Because he already said no."

Her expression turns stormy. "He did what?" She huffs. "Didn't I raise that boy right?"

"No, Ma'am," Davis replies unhelpfully. "Can't say you did."

Eyes narrow, she glares at him, then taps a finger against her chin. "Unfortunately, I'm tied up with work at the moment, but I'm sure Davis could show you around tomorrow. Sunday is his day off."

Davis's handsome face creases in a smile. "Hell yeah, I can."

I glance from one of them to the other, wondering what they're playing at. A moment ago, she was warning him off, but now she's volunteering his services. What am I missing?

"Are you sure that's okay?" I ask him. "I'd hate to put you out."

"It's no problem at all. What better way to spend my off-day than with a beautiful woman? I can pick you up for brunch, if that suits."

"Brunch sounds perfect. Thank you so much." I give them both a little wave. "I don't want to hold you up, so I'll be going. See you then."

"Bye, Felicity," Nadine calls as I walk back to the car. "Don't give up on Wyatt. He has a good heart under his surliness."

Shaking my head, I wonder what planet she's living on. Whether or not Wyatt has a good heart has nothing to do with me—he's made that clear. I head back to the rental, but when I arrive, I pause and go to Wyatt's place instead of mine. I knock firmly on his front door.

"I haven't changed my mind," he says as he yanks it open. No greeting, no nothing. Then, I get a good look at him and swallow. He's wearing gym shorts and a sleeveless tank that perfectly showcases his massive biceps. Seriously, those arms are as thick as my legs.

"I know," I say. "I just wanted to say that the cookies are a gift, not a bribe. I found someone else who can show me around."

He leans against the doorframe and crosses his arms over his chest. The muscles bulge, and I have a hard time looking away from them. "Who?"

Dragging my gaze up to his face, I reply, "Just someone who was landscaping at your mom's place when I went to visit."

His brow furrows. "You visited my mom?"

"Yeah." I link my hands behind my back to stop them from fidgeting. "To ask her to help me out."

"Wait." The groove between his eyebrows deepens. "Not Davis Gentry?"

"Yeah, that's him." Of course they know each other. Most likely everyone in Oak Bend knows everyone else. "We're having brunch tomorrow."

"And *Mom* is the one who suggested that?" he demands.

I nod and his face is a mask of shock, but then he wipes the expression off.

"Good luck with that."

What's *that* supposed to mean? Clearly something is going on here that I don't know about.

"Why are you so surprised?" I ask, shifting my weight from one foot to the other.

He gives me a searching look. "Because it's not like Mom to feed sweet young women to the wolves."

I burst out laughing. I can't help it. "You're being a bit over dramatic."

"You wouldn't say that if you knew Davis the way I do," he grumbles. "He eats girls like you for breakfast."

"Or brunch," I offer, trying to reign in the giggles. He doesn't look amused. "He's a flirt. I get it. I appreciate you warning me, but I noticed that all on my own and I'm not worried about him." I take a step back. "I just wanted to let you know you're off the hook."

"But you're on it."

I cover my mouth to hide my smile. He's too adorable when he's being pouty. "Thanks for your concern, but I can take care of myself." I wiggle my fingers at him. "Bye for now.

"Don't believe a word the guy says," he yells after me.

Wyatt

WHAT DOES Mom think she's playing at?

Davis may be one of my closest friends, but he's a total playboy. And Felicity is prime pickings—sweet, naive, and pretty. I go to the kitchen and shove another of those chocolate chip cookies into my mouth because she's also an excellent baker.

Damn Mom. She's only doing this to wind me up. She's probably disappointed that her plan hasn't worked out, and she's trying to back me into a corner. She knows I have a protective streak a mile wide and won't want Davis anywhere near my new neighbor. My phone sits on the kitchen counter, and I snatch it up and send her a text message.

Wyatt: *Stop playing games.*

She responds so quickly that I can't help but think she's been waiting for me to reach out.

Mom: *No idea what you mean.*

Wyatt: *Why would you introduce Davis to Felicity? You know how he is.*

Mom: *They'd already met. I just suggested he help her out. She is new in town, after all.*

Wyatt: *She doesn't need his kind of help.*

Mom: *Isn't that for her to decide?*

I drag a hand through my hair and sigh. She makes a good point, but I have a feeling Felicity is the kind of person to trust others wholeheartedly until they prove her wrong. And much as I don't want anything to do with her, I'd hate for her to get hurt.

Wyatt: *She might take his flirting seriously.*

Except she gave the impression she knew better than that, so why am I pissed off by the thought of them together?

Mom: *He was quite taken with her, and she's a smart girl. She can take care of herself. Don't worry about them. Everything is fine. Why do you care anyway?*

"I don't," I mutter to myself and tell her goodbye. Time to try another tactic. I'll be seeing Davis soon for our casual Saturday basketball game. I can talk to him then.

When I arrive at the court, the man in question is chatting up a pair of brunettes who look like sisters. I join the other guys, not in the mood to listen to him charm women.

"Hey, man," Miles greets as I approach. At well over six feet with Native American heritage, he usually attracts just as much female attention as Davis, if not more. The difference is, he doesn't particularly want it, while Davis revels in it.

I clap him on the shoulder. "Been a while."

"Yeah, I've been busy with the renovations."

I nod. He and his brothers are restoring one of the larger houses near the center of town after inheriting it from an uncle. "How are they coming along?"

"Kitchen is done. Living areas too. Just working on the bedrooms and the exterior now." He raises a hand as two of our friends approach. "We expecting many today?"

I shrug. "Davis would know."

At that moment, Davis breaks away from the brunettes and saunters over to join us.

"Wyatt," he exclaims. "You've been holding out on me. Your neighbor sure is a looker."

"She's not your type," I snap.

He raises his eyebrows at my biting tone. "Beautiful is my type, and she's most definitely that."

"She's a writer," I counter. "Too smart for you."

He flashes a grin. "Nerds are hot. I banged plenty of them in high school. How do you think I graduated?"

I roll my eyes, because any stronger reaction would give away too much. He doesn't need to know I find Felicity attractive. That would only make things worse.

"Who's this?" Miles asks, glancing from me to Davis.

"The hottie who moved in next to Wyatt," Davis replies. "Felicity. Cute blonde with fantastic tits and—"

"That's enough," I thunder, not wanting to hear what the 'and' is.

"And a really nice smile," he finishes, ignoring me. To Miles, he says, "I get to be her tour guide, thanks to Nadine. Just think of all the chances I'll have to—"

"No, you won't," I snap, the final frayed end of my temper breaking. "Because *I'm* the one who's going to show her around. She deserves better than to be hit on nonstop."

Davis's eyes glitter with amusement. "Have it your way."

"I will." Crossing my arms over my chest, I scowl. He looks far too self-satisfied. If I didn't know better, I'd think he and Mom had conspired against me. Surely not.

Anyway, I'm committed now. It doesn't have to be a big deal. I can take Felicity around the local attractions in one afternoon, and then I don't have to see her again. It's worth it to keep her safe from the local player. I may not want her next door, but I don't want her to be used and tossed aside either.

Yeah, that's definitely why I snapped at Davis. It has nothing to do with jealousy or the red haze of fury that descends when I think of him touching her. I'm a protector. I keep the women in my life safe. That's all this is.

"You all right?" Miles asks, concern in his voice.

"Fine." Although I can't help feeling like I've been expertly manipulated. Belatedly, it occurs to me to hope Felicity won't mind the change of plan.

CHAPTER 4

FELICITY

THE BIRDS ARE SINGING when I knock on Wyatt's door on Sunday morning, my nerves a riot and a brownie tin tucked under my arm. When he dropped by last night to advise me of the change in plans, I have to admit, I was relieved. While any guide would be nice, I much prefer Wyatt to Davis. Maybe he's gruff and broody, but he has depths. Davis is clearly a flirt—his personality is out there for anyone to see—whereas Wyatt is a mystery, and I want to know what makes him tick. Yeah, that's one of the more annoying aspects of my personality: the need to look under the hood. Hopefully, he'll come to accept my friendship. Luckily, growing up rootless means I learned that the fastest way to make friends is to offer gifts. Hence the brownies.

He opens the door and blinks down at me sleepily, then rubs his eyes, the movement drawing his t-shirt tight across his muscled torso.

"Don't tell me." His voice is rough from disuse, and a niggle at the back of my mind warns me I've woken him. "You're a morning person?"

I resist the urge to check the time, knowing it's at least

nine. "Um, yeah. Dawn is when I get my best words written."

"Dawn, huh?" His expression shutters, but I have no idea why. "Even on a Sunday?"

"I write every day." Sensing that his mood hangs in a precarious balance, I thrust the tin at him. "I made you brownies."

He examines it, bemused. "They're still warm."

"Only came out of the oven twenty minutes ago."

He shakes his head. "You did get an early start." He raises the tin to his nose and sniffs. "Fuck, these smell good. Mind if I have one?"

"They're for you."

He turns and lumbers inside. Assuming I'm supposed I follow, I trail behind, seeing the parts of the house I didn't on Friday. We pass a spare bedroom and what must be the master bedroom, judging by the unmade bed. It strikes me as strange that he chooses to sleep in a smaller room, but I don't ask about it because I do have some boundaries.

The living room is comfortably arranged, with a faded couch in its center, facing a coffee table and television. There's a small desk in one corner, an ancient laptop perched on top, along with enough receipts to fuel a fire. The kitchen, however, is familiar, which makes me feel less like I'm intruding as he places the tin on the counter and dishes two generous pieces of brownie onto small plates. He hands me one, paired with a dessert fork, and claims the other for himself. We eat in companionable silence, except for the noises of enjoyment that rumble from Wyatt's throat. I love those sounds. I could listen to them all day. There's nothing sexier than watching an attractive man make verbal love to his food.

"That's delicious," he says after wiping his mouth on a

29

napkin. "Almost makes the early morning worth it. I'd pay for that."

"Yay!" I beam, my heart lifting. "Good thing you don't have to because you have your own free supply next door."

He chuckles, and I feel an answering tremor in my belly. His laugh is almost as good as his food appreciation noises. Deep, warm, and gentle. "Don't make promises you can't keep, or I'll be turning up on your doorstep every night."

"That wouldn't be so bad."

His eyes linger on me, growing heated, and I squirm. But then just as quickly, he glances away and ends the moment.

"So, where's the best place to go for brunch?" I ask.

"If you like greasy spoon food, it's Mickey's Diner."

I nod. "I had dinner there last night. Great cheeseburger. Massive, though. Do they do waffles or pancakes?"

"Yes to waffles, no to pancakes."

"Perfect. Waffles, it is." I stand and make it a few steps before I notice he isn't following. "Aren't you coming?"

He collects the plates and puts them in his sink. "Wasn't planning to."

"Oh." Wait—had I not invited him? No, I hadn't. "Please come. I'd love to eat with you."

He sighs and turns back to me. "I'm not a brunch kind of guy."

"But you like waffles," I prompt, walking over to him. "Everyone likes waffles."

"Actually, everyone doesn't."

My face falls.

"But I do," he adds, heaving another sigh.

"Come and have some waffles," I say. "Then, we can start our tour."

He looks uncertain, and it bothers me. That sliver of doubt slices the inside of my gut. The doubting voice that says I can't force people to like me, no matter how hard I try, and I'll always be an outsider wherever I go.

"Please."

My desperation must reflect in my expression, because his shoulders slump and he nods. "Okay, just give me a moment to change."

"You look great in those sweatpants."

He arches a brow. Ugh, why did I say that? He probably knows exactly how delectable he is, and now I've given away the fact I'm not immune to him.

"I'll be two minutes." He brushes past me, and I make myself comfortable in the living room, taking the chance to look around. On the desk is a framed photograph of a younger Wyatt with Nadine and another woman. His girlfriend? He hasn't mentioned one, and Nadine's comments would lead me to believe he's single. An ex perhaps? Or maybe a sister? I forgot to ask whether he has siblings. I'll have to remedy that soon.

When he emerges, he's wearing faded jeans that hug his thighs perfectly and a white t-shirt that molds to his chest and abs. My mouth dries. Whatever he does, it keeps him in excellent physical shape.

"What's your job?" I ask.

He cocks his head. "I'm a brick mason, remember? Why?"

"No reason." My cheeks heat, and I hope I'm not as red as I feel. But now the image of a shirtless Wyatt hauling around lumps of stone, every muscle straining, has infiltrated my mind, and I can't get it out.

"Come on." He jerks his chin toward the door. "Let's go."

I scurry after him and start toward my car, but he grabs

my arm to stop me. Where his fingers touch my skin, I feel it *everywhere*.

"I'm not going anywhere in your tiny little car," he says. "We'll take my truck."

Wyatt's truck is one of the type tradesmen often use, with a covered trailer attached and tools scattered throughout. He clears a toolbox off the passenger seat, and I climb up.

"So, you're a brick mason," I say as he starts the engine. "Any siblings?"

"Just my sister," he replies. "Julia."

"What about your dad?"

He glances over, expression stony. "What about him?"

I gulp. Perhaps I shouldn't have asked. "Is he... around?"

"No. He and Mom divorced when I was little, and I've seen him only a couple of times since then."

"I'm sorry."

He shrugs but doesn't say anything more.

After a tense thirty seconds, I offer some information of my own. "I don't know my dad at all."

"Oh?" He glances over, and I can't tell whether he's interested or just grateful for the reprieve.

"He was some guy my mom slept with a few times. She was always on the lookout for love, and it never went anywhere." Even now, she still picks up her life and moves across the country every few months because she's met someone new. I'm just glad she can't drag me along anymore.

"That must have been hard."

Now it's my turn to shrug. What can I say? It messed me up. Now all I want is routine and stability, but thanks to her, I seem to lack the social skills and emotional sturdiness to create a long-term home.

"Have you always lived in Oak Bend?" The change of topic isn't subtle, but I don't much care.

He exhales and shakes his head. "You ask a lot of questions."

I quieten because he's right—I do. And people don't always like it, but I can't help wanting to know.

As we pull up outside the diner, he nods. "Yeah. I'm a Bender, born and bred."

I smile, to show my thanks. We head inside, and the same redhead that served me last night is behind the counter.

"Mornin', Madge." Wyatt greets her with a smile that's more genuine than any I've seen from him so far. "Having a good one?"

"Crazy," she replies, blowing a strand of hair out of her eyes. "Every trucker and his dog turned up this morning." Her gaze tracks from him to me and lights with curiosity. "I see you've met our newest import."

"Of course." His tone is wry. "Mom made sure to send her over immediately."

Madge laughs. "Can't say no to your momma, kid."

"Tell me about it."

She gives me a once-over. "What can I get you, hon?"

"Waffles, please."

She glances at Wyatt.

"Same for me, and some fried chicken."

"Chicken waffles." She nods but doesn't make a note of it.

Wyatt dips his head closer to mine. "Madge remembers everything."

Her eyes narrow. "Including when you skinny-dipped in my swimming pool."

33

He sticks his hands into his pockets and seems to shrink an inch. "I was ten."

"You were a horror." She tuts. "Take your girl to the table in the corner, and the food will be over soon. Coffee?"

"Yes, please."

I follow him to the table she's indicated, and we sit. We've been there for all of two minutes before an older lady with gray hair and round spectacles approaches.

"Wyatt Dawson," she says as she reaches us. "I can't believe you haven't introduced me to your friend. I hear she's a writer."

"We've just gotten here," he grouses. "I haven't even had a chance to get a drink, let alone make introductions."

"Hi." I smile. She has this look about her that suggests she spoils her grandchildren rotten and has never said a mean word in her life. "I'm Felicity."

"And I'm Sherry," she replies. "The local librarian."

"I love libraries! They're absolutely magical."

Sherry preens, visibly proud of what she does. "They are that."

"I'm going to need to scope out some new places to write. I'll have to come by and look around." Libraries and coffee shops are my favorite places to work. While I can write anywhere, including home, I seem to be more productive when I'm surrounded by inspiration.

"I hope you'll do more than that," she says, lowering herself onto a chair beside me without waiting for an invitation. "I'd love for you to come and do a reading."

I blink at her, nonplussed. "But you don't even know what I write. It could be erotica."

Sherry winks. "So much the better."

Wyatt snorts but doesn't say anything when she gives him a sharp look.

"What do you write, Felicity?"

"Horror." Somehow, I manage to imbue the word with a bravado I don't feel.

She claps, apparently delighted. "Perfect! The girls will love it."

"Girls?"

She smooths down a fluffy tuft of hair. "The genre fiction book club. We read romance, mysteries and thrillers, horror, all the good stuff." She waves a hand. "I know people expect librarians to be literary snobs, but that's way too much hard work. I prefer to enjoy my books."

Reaching over, I take her hand. "I would be honored to do a reading for you. I think we're going to get along famously."

Wyatt

EVERYONE AROUND TOWN LOVES FELICITY. Of course they do. She's sweet, enthusiastic, and has an unconscious charm that draws people to her. Of course, people love gossip, too, and word will be all over Oak Bend by nightfall that I have a new love interest. I'm certainly not saying that I do, but that's how the locals will spin it. It's a widely known secret that I've been single since the night I walked in and found Dawn screwing another man in our bed—not because I shared the story with anyone who asked, but because *she* did. My ex loves attention, good or bad. In any case, the news I've been spotted with a pretty blonde will spread quickly, which is exactly what Mom probably hopes for.

Despite that, I can't bring myself to be short with

Felicity or to hold her accountable. She doesn't know how this town works, and she's too endearing to blame. But even though she's nice, the woman can talk. Goddamn, can she *talk*. For ten minutes, she babbles a non-stop stream of excitement about the library's genre fiction book club, and then she oohs and aahs over the waffles, which are good but hardly worthy of the praise she heaps upon them. After we finish brunch, she asks me to escort her around the popular shops and eateries, and now here we are, outside the library. She's flitted in and out of nearly every building in the commercial area but wanted to save the best for last.

"It's gorgeous!" she exclaims. "Oh, my God. The arches. The windows. Those gothic vibes." She turns to me, eyes shining. "It's perfect." Then, she reaches for the handle and pulls. It doesn't open.

"Damn," I mutter. Unfortunately, I'd forgotten it would be closed on a Sunday. Her expression falls, making me feel like I kicked her puppy. "Sorry." I shrug. "I don't really use the library, so I don't know the operating hours."

Her jaw drops. "But libraries are the cornerstone of a community!"

I can't help but chuckle. "Have you ever heard of eBooks? They don't require a membership card, and you can access them anywhere."

She huffs, and cocks a hip, placing her hand on it. "Yes, and I love them, but they don't have the same atmosphere as a library. Libraries are where you meet book lovers who share your passion. Plus," she points a finger in the air with her free hand, "they smell like old books."

I grin. She's fiery when it comes to books. Noted. "Eh. I can take or leave the old book smell."

"Oh, my God." She spins away as if she can't bear to look at me, then turns back, her skirt flouncing around her knees.

"I can't believe what I'm hearing. Who doesn't love old book smell? It's the best thing ever."

"I thought libraries were the best thing ever?"

She gasps, her hand going to her mouth, but then her eyes narrow. "You're having me on."

My lips twitch. "Am I?"

They narrow further, forming slits, and it's actually kind of adorable. "Yes," she declares, with confidence. "You are, because *every* reader loves old book smell."

"Okay," I relent. "You got me."

"That's right, I did." Her smile is smug, and when she playfully shoves my arm, a zing of something jolts through me.

Desire.

It's an emotion I haven't experienced in what feels like ages, and that's the way I like it. I flinch away from her, and her forehead crinkles in confusion.

"Well, that's it," I announce. "The tour is over. I better get home; I have work to do around the house."

"But..." She trails off. "Oh, okay then. I guess I've taken up enough of your Sunday. Will you give me a ride back?"

"I drove you here, didn't I?" My tone is snappier than I intend.

Her expression darkens, and her shoulders hunch in on themselves. My gut contracts because I know I'm being an ass, but I need to get away from her. To put some distance between us. Honestly, even though I've done manual labor all week, it seems like a safer idea than spending more time with her. Better to work the energy out of my system than let Felicity worm her way under my skin.

"Come on, the truck is over here."

CHAPTER 5

FELICITY

On Monday morning, I take my laptop to the local coffee shop, Java by Jackie, which Wyatt showed me yesterday. It's in a refurbished building on the town square. The interior walls are distressed brick, and as I enter, I glance up at the exposed wooden beams of the ceiling. While the shop isn't particularly wide, it's long, and I can see a perfect spot in the back corner to sit and write.

"Hi," I say as I approach the counter.

The woman behind it, who's maybe a few years younger than me, glances up from a book she's been engrossed in. "Can I help you?"

I gesture at the book. "What are you reading?"

She runs a hand through her short pixie cut and shows me the spine. The words "Nineteen Eighty-Four" are printed along it.

"Oh, you like the classics?"

"Love them." She smiles shyly. "You must be the author everyone is talking about."

I wince. "They are?"

"Don't take it personally. That's just how this town is."

She places a bookmark between the pages and sets Orwell aside. "I'm Ella."

"Felicity," I reply. "I'm actually looking for a place to work." I hold up the laptop. "Do you mind if I take one of the tables in the back? I promise to drink plenty of coffee."

"Go ahead." She scans the three patrons who are already here—all of whom are watching us. "You'll probably be good for business. Can I get you anything for breakfast?"

I check the range of pastries and slices in the cabinet. "I'll have a blueberry Danish, please."

"Perfect."

I go to pay, but she shakes her head. "If you're going to be here for a while, I'll run a tab and you can pay it all at the end."

"Are you sure?"

She nods. "Go make your magic."

A smile spreads over my face. Today is going to be great, I just know it. Already it's off to such a good start. The people of Oak Bend are lovely—even if I don't quite understand the stoic brick mason. I choose one of the smaller tables and open my laptop, then tab to the story I've been working on, about a young couple who seek refuge from a storm in a haunted abbey. Picking up where I left off yesterday, I sink into the world I've created, a place where I can be as twisted as I want and readers love it. I used to wonder if there was something wrong with my mind because the darkest stories were the ones I loved most, but I've come to see that what I truly adore is knowing that a thread of hope carries through. No matter how many people die horrifically along the way, someone always emerges from the darkness intact—even if it's only the character's beloved dog. For some reason, that really speaks to me.

I'm halfway through a scene in which the couple are

fleeing along a stone corridor when a voice at the adjacent table breaks my concentration. Mildly annoyed, I look over. A woman with a white bob—or is it pale blonde?—is waving her hands at Ella, although not in an angry way. She's slender, and despite the fact she's resting her elbows on the table, she gives the impression of being tall. Straining my ears, I try to pick up the thread of their conversation. "It's a disaster," the woman with the bob announces.

"Now, Christine, I'm sure it's not that bad," Ella soothes, her eyes darting around to make sure no one is being disturbed. She catches me watching and one of her brows lifts, but she turns her attention back to Christine. "No one else runs a town with as much precision as you do. Oak Bend is a well-oiled machine. I just know you'll find someone perfect to plan the festival and it will be even better than last year."

Christine heaves a sigh. "I thought you were supposed to be the voice of reason. You're heaping even more pressure on me."

I stick up my hand like I'm in school, waiting for the teacher to call on me. I don't know why I've done it, and frankly, it's a little embarrassing when both women turn my way.

Christine flicks her analytical gaze over me. "You must be Felicity."

I gape. "How does everyone know my name?"

"We don't get many young, pretty writers around these parts. Especially not famous ones."

"You Googled me?" I'm not sure whether to be flattered or horrified. I mean, I've written a couple of bestsellers, but I'm no Stephen King.

She smiles, and it's one of those true smiles that crinkles the corners of her eyes. "I take my position as mayor of Oak

Bend very seriously, which means doing my due diligence on each of our residents. I hear you're friendly with Wyatt Dawson."

I cover a grimace. "I don't think he likes me very much. He only showed me around because his mom bullied him into it."

Her smile softens. "The thing you need to know about Wyatt is that he doesn't do anything he doesn't want to. The man is stubborn as a ram. He just doesn't know how to enjoy himself anymore. He's been a hermit ever since..." She coughs to mask the way she trails off, and darned if I don't want to know whatever she was about to say. "The point is, he likes you just fine. Now, is there a reason you're waiting to be called on like a child."

My cheeks heat as blood rushes to them. "What were you saying about a festival?"

"The annual Fall Harvest and Craft Festival," Ella interjects, rolling a pen between her fingers. "The organizer has stepped down because she's moving out of town. The trouble is, it's in three weeks, so Christine is having a meltdown because she doesn't think it's possible to find a replacement and get everything sorted out in time."

"I'll do it." The offer is out of my mouth before I've thought it through.

Both women stare at me.

"Have you ever planned a festival?" Christine asks.

"No, but I've been on the committee for a school fundraiser." Despite not having any children. I'm great at signing up for things. Perhaps a little less great at executing on them, if I'm honest.

"Thank you, honey, but it's a completely different thing."

Ella swats Christine's arm. "Chris, what are you doing?"

she hisses. "If someone offers to do the very thing you're stressing about, you say 'yes, thank you so much for taking it off my plate.'"

Christine sighs and eyes me, as though trying to determine whether I'm competent by x-ray visioning through my exterior. It's slightly unnerving. "Thank you, Felicity. That's a very kind offer, but planning the festival is a big commitment. Are you sure you'll have the time?"

"Absolutely. I'll make it happen." It's as if this opportunity has been dropped in my lap by the universe. What better way to prove I belong here and to integrate myself into the community than by planning a festival for everyone to enjoy? I can already picture it. Walking between stalls as people stop me to thank me on bringing such a lovely event together.

She still looks uncertain. "You don't know the town."

"We can help her with that," Ella says. "There is no shortage of people who could talk her through it. They just don't want to do the work themselves."

I'm on tenterhooks, awaiting Christine's verdict.

"Okay." She smiles, and her face relaxes. "I truly appreciate it, and we'll make sure you have the support you need."

"Why don't you join me, and tell me all about it?" I suggest.

She nods. "I'll do that."

Wyatt

I HEFT a brick into place and make sure it's perfectly aligned, then reach for another. I've been working on Mrs. Bainbridge's brick fence with my buddy Steve since dawn—

mostly without speaking as we listen to music from a boom-box. Steve sits on the ground and drinks from his water bottle.

"So," he says, setting the bottle down and mopping his forehead with the hem of his shirt. "Tell me about the new girl."

"Not sure who you mean," I reply, knowing exactly who he means.

He rolls his eyes, seeing my fib for what it is. "The girl next door. Nadine's new project. I hear she's pretty."

I grunt and place the brick where it's meant to go.

"Wy, you know I don't talk gorilla. Is she a looker? Nice? Available?"

I keep working because if I pause to have this conversation, I won't escape it anytime soon. "What do you care?"

He grabs a protein bar from his pocket. "Not a lot of women our age around these parts. I'd like to meet her."

I snort. "She's the type you settle down with."

"And?" He raises a brow. "Maybe I'm ready to settle down. We're thirty. Our days of running wild are over. I want more."

His statement unsettles me. I'd thought I was ready to settle down, and look how that turned out. I'd hate for the same thing to happen to him.

"Come on," he pleads. "Throw me a bone. I just want to know a little about her."

My chest heavy, I drop to the ground beside him and stretch my legs out. "She's pretty. Sweet. Late twenties, probably. I haven't seen any sign of a boyfriend."

"Would I like her?"

"Probably," I admit. "There's a lot to like."

Steve's eyes narrow. "Do *you* like her? Because I don't want to encroach."

"Nah, man." I give a slight shake of my head. "Not my type. But I can ask if she wants the local assholes hitting on her."

He grins. "Appreciate it."

The rest of the day passes with no further mention of Felicity, and by the time I get home and find her kneeling in the front garden, sifting through the flowerbed, I've all but forgotten my promise to Steve.

"Hi, Wyatt!" She wipes her palms on the grass to remove loose dirt and leaps to her feet. My eyes drink her in. Even while she gardens, she's wearing a bright skirt and her lips are painted pink. She smiles, and her eyes twinkle in a way that makes me feel like an old stodge because there's just so much life in her.

"Hey."

She steps forward, trips, and catches herself, a blush rising up her cheeks. "You'll never guess what happened today."

"No, I probably won't," I concede. Her smile droops, and I realize she wants me to ask about it. What's more, I'm tired and don't have it in me to pretend I don't notice. "So tell me."

She perks up again. "I'm going to plan the Fall Harvest and Craft Festival. The woman who was planning it is leaving, and I overheard Christine talking to Ella about it and offered to help."

"Whoa, whoa." I hold up a hand. "Slow your roll. Did you just say you're planning the festival?"

"Yep." She beams. "You're looking at Oak Bend's newest festival planner."

I gulp. Joy practically radiates from her pores. How is it possible for one woman to shine so much on the inside?

"You've only just moved here. It's in three weeks."

She raises her chin, expression surprisingly stubborn. "Plenty of time. Have a little faith, Wyatt. Things will work out."

I don't answer, because in my experience that isn't usually the case.

"Gosh." Her nose crinkles. "You're such a spoilsport. I'm going to make the best festival the town has ever seen, just you wait."

I groan because she's clearly deluded as well as impulsive, but her heart is in a good place. "Do you understand what you've signed yourself up for?"

"Not yet." She shrugs. "But I will soon. Once I've finished in the garden, I'm going to do some research. I was hoping you might tell me a bit more about it from a local's perspective."

I sigh. Of course she was. "I suppose I could do that."

"Thanks." Her smile is impish, but there's a steeliness beneath it that's strangely appealing. Perhaps there's more to Felicity Bell than I believed. "Can I come over in half an hour?"

"Fine." I may as well just accept that she'll be nosing around in my life until she rolls out of town again. Because it *is* a matter of 'when,' not 'if.' From what she's told me, she never stays in one place for more than a year, and perhaps she wants that to change but people don't. Not at the core. She'll be out of here again soon enough.

"You're the best." She reaches out to hug me, but I step back, dodging her. "Not a hugger?"

She looks disappointed, and I feel like a dick. But if she touches me, I'm afraid I won't want her to stop, and I can't become attached to someone I know will leave. I've been naive in the past, and I've learned from that mistake.

"Nope."

She tilts her head to the side, studying me without speaking for a moment. "Back to the one-word replies."

"I'm not much of a talker." If she wants conversations and heart-to-hearts, she'll be disappointed, just as Dawn was. "See you soon." I turn to walk away.

As I stride up the stairs, I hear her call after me. "You're wrong, you know. You like to talk; you just won't let yourself."

I ignore her. I have to, for my own sake. I can't afford to dwell on whether she might be right. Instead, I head for the shower and wash away the dust and grime from a long day of manual labor. When I emerge, towel around my waist, and peer out the window, Felicity is still in the garden. Based on the pile of discarded plants growing beside her, she clearly has no idea what she's doing. But she's dedicated to the task, and I can't help but admire that. It's been a long time since my heart was in anything.

CHAPTER 6

FELICITY

I'm at the same table as yesterday in the rear of the coffee shop, midway through a scene in which the young couple are hiding behind a door while footsteps pace outside when someone pulls out the chair opposite me. I flinch, the movement jarring me out of deep concentration, and glance up. A statuesque blonde sinks onto the chair and folds one tanned leg over the other. She looks me up and down, a decidedly judgmental gleam in her eye.

"So, you're the writer."

"Ah, yes. That's me." Not that I have any idea who *she* is.

She cocks her head. "You're not what I expected."

"I'm sorry?"

"I mean, you're not much to look at, are you?"

My mouth drops open.

"I guess you don't have to be glamorous to write about death and gore."

"Excuse me?" I squeak, looking around to see if anyone else is as shocked by what's going on as I am. I catch the gaze of a woman a couple of tables over, whose dark hair is

47

in a ponytail down her back, a ball cap pulled low over her face. She shakes her head at the blonde, who ignores us both, her upper lip curling into a sneer that warps her beautiful face into something meaner.

"I don't get what everyone's so excited about." She tuts. "It's not as if you've won a Pulitzer."

"I haven't," I agree, glancing at my blinking cursor with longing as I realize she's not going anywhere. "I'm just a girl who likes to tell stories."

Her eyes narrow. "I hope you don't expect your story to have a happy ending here in Oak Bend."

I sit up straighter. "I'm sorry, but I have no idea what you're talking about."

She perches her elbow on the table and rests her chin on her palm. "Your love life." She rolls her eyes as though it should be obvious. "With the happily ever after reference and being a writer, I thought for sure you'd get that, but maybe you're not as clever as people make you out to be."

Scanning the tables again, I notice that people are watching us. The brunette in the ball cap mouths words, but I can't tell what. All I know is there's something at play here I'm not aware of.

"Look," I say. "I don't know who you are or why you think my personal life is your business, but perhaps I can ease your mind. I don't have a love life at the moment. At all." I smile even though I'd rather ask her to leave. "Nada."

"Good." She returns my smile, displaying far too many teeth, the expression catty rather than friendly. "Keep it that way."

Something in her tone piques my interest. "Out of curiosity, what's this about?"

For a moment, I think she won't answer, but then she says, "Wyatt."

Ah, so this is about Wyatt. I nod to myself. Is she his girlfriend? Because I didn't think he had one, but then, I've been wrong before.

"You have absolutely no need to worry," I assure her. "Wyatt is my next-door neighbor, and I hope we're building a friendship of sorts, but I have no designs on him." However scrumptious and broody he may be.

She leans forward. "Perfect." Her lips form a moue as she scans me up and down. "I should have known you weren't his type." She stands and stares down at me. "Catch you later, writer girl."

With that, she flounces off, and I stare after her, agape. As she exits the store, the woman in the ball cap makes her way over to me.

"You okay?" she asks. "Dawn can be a bit much."

"Yeah, I guess so." I run a hand over my hair, refusing to acknowledge when my fingers tremble. "Is she Wyatt's girlfriend or something?"

"Ex," she clarifies.

"Oh." Even though I suspected something along those lines, my heart sinks. I hadn't wanted to believe that she was his type. I was hoping he preferred bookworms who talk too much.

She extends a hand. "I'm CJ."

"Felicity."

Her grip is firm, and she smirks. "I know."

"Of course you do." I have to laugh. It seems like everyone around here knows my business better than I do. "Dawn and Wyatt seem like an unusual couple. Have they been separated for long?"

CJ shrugs. "Six months, but they were together for two years or so before that. I think it's a sore point for both of them."

"What happened?" I ask, wanting to understand him better.

Her phone rings, and she fishes it out of her pocket. "Damn. I have to go, sorry."

I nod, feeling like I've been handed enough pieces of a jigsaw to get an idea of the image but not enough to put it together. As I'm a nosy person by nature, it's frustrating.

"It was nice to meet you."

"You, too."

As I watch her go, I ponder the fact that at least now I know where I stand with Wyatt. Anyone who dated a woman like Dawn won't be interested in me. She's glamorous, effortlessly beautiful, and has probably been breaking hearts since junior high. Me, on the other hand? I've always been an outsider who tries too hard to fit in. My twisted mind freaks people out.

I sigh, disappointed despite myself. I really wouldn't have picked Dawn as Wyatt's type. I didn't think he'd have the patience for drama, and she screams high maintenance. But then, what do I know about him?

Nothing.

Perhaps he's gorgeous and broody and I want to lick him like an ice cream, but I don't know him, and I have no claim on him. With a shake of my head, I return to writing. It's time for someone to die. Coincidentally, my pretty young heroine—the one who's about to meet an untimely end— bears a startling resemblance to the woman I just met.

Wyatt

I'VE JUST SAT down for my lunch break, legs sprawled in front of me on the grass, and pulled a sandwich from my bag when I see the pink convertible coming my way. Dawn's car mirrors her self-image. Shiny and expensive. Her father has plenty of money and loves to spend it making her happy. I used to think that was sweet, but now I see the effect it has on her—the way it makes her believe she can have whatever she wants without facing the consequences. She pulls over to the side of the road and kills the engine, then swings out of the driver's seat in a movement so casually elegant it used to drive me crazy. It still does, but not in a good way. It's fake. Practiced.

Then, I spot the brown paper bag tucked under her arm.

"Hi, handsome," she says as she rounds the car. "Hard at work?"

"How did you find me?" I ask.

She shrugs. "People talk."

Of course they do. One of the few downsides of Oak Bend.

"I brought you lunch." She offers me the bag. "Chicken on rye."

I hold up my sandwich. "I'm covered."

Her upper lip curls. "This is better. Trust me."

I snort. "Trust you? No, thanks. Look where that got me last time."

She cringes, but I don't feel the least bit sorry for her. She brought any discomfort she's experiencing on herself. "You know it was a mistake. I miss you. Can we at least sit together while you eat and talk about it?"

"No." I take a bite of my sandwich even though it tastes like sawdust in my mouth and chew slowly, hoping she'll leave. When she doesn't, I swallow before continuing.

"Every time I look at you, all I can see is the image of Brody fucking you in our bed. Nothing is gonna happen between us ever again."

"But Wy—" She breaks off, eyes narrowing, and then, before I have time to react, she ducks and smacks a kiss onto my forehead. I jerk back, shocked, and follow the direction of her gaze all the way to Felicity, who is staring at us from the other side of the street, a laptop case slung over her shoulder. Dawn's smile turns smug, and she curls her finger-nails into my shoulder like a lioness claiming its kill. Felicity tears her gaze from us and fixes it on a point in the distance. She carries on as though she never noticed us at all, but her focus is a little too determined.

I see what Dawn is doing. She's heard that I'm spending time with another woman, and she's marking her territory. Fucking hell. I rake a hand through my hair. I want to run after Felicity and tell her that she's got it wrong. I'm not the slightest bit interested in my unfaithful ex, but because I care enough about my neighbor to not want her upset, I don't give chase. Sounds stupid, I know, but I need to keep my distance. And if she thinks I'm unavailable, it'll be easier to do that. Besides, I shouldn't encourage her when I can't offer her anything. No relationship or happily ever after. I don't have it in me to be a good boyfriend—Dawn has convinced me of that—and I can't handle spending time with someone romantically only to have them come to the same conclusion. Especially a woman as sweet as Felicity. I couldn't take the eventual rejection.

CHAPTER 7

FELICITY

CLEARLY, I was wrong about Dawn not being Wyatt's type. Her hands are all over him, and he doesn't seem to mind in the slightest. I keep walking, ignoring the wobble of my lower lip. He means nothing to me. I have a teensy crush on him, that's all. He and Dawn have history, and besides, any man who is attracted to her surely wouldn't find much to like about me. We're both blonde, but I'm short where she's tall. I'm all colors and noise, while she seems sleek and stylish. I guess it's for the best that I met her now, before I could get too interested in my handsome neighbor.

I arrive home, grab the pastry I bought for lunch, and open my laptop on the table while I eat. This morning, I talked to a few of the locals about the Fall Harvest and Craft Festival, and now I'm feeling more confident in what's involved. Of course, knowing and doing are two different things, but I feel like I've made a good first step. I open an empty document and start brainstorming what I need to do next. I have a meeting scheduled with Christine tomorrow, which will clarify things, but I want to go into it prepared.

The rest of the week passes with mornings spent

writing and afternoons occupied by planning. A picture starts to form within my mind, and I'm feeling good about the festival. Each evening, I take leftover dessert next door to share with Wyatt. He doesn't talk much, but he hasn't sent me packing either. Much as he may grumble, his sweet tooth won't let him say no to sugar—even if it comes with company attached. He hasn't said anything about Dawn, and I haven't asked. Frankly, it's not my business, and I don't want to know.

On Friday, I turn up on his doorstep with two thick slices of apple pie. He opens the door before I even knock and inhales deeply.

"Mm, smells good. Apple and cinnamon?"

"Pie," I confirm and hand him the container.

His stomach growls, and he ducks his head sheepishly. "Haven't eaten yet."

"Let's get this pie into you, then." I bustle inside, pretending not to notice the fact he hasn't invited me in.

"Do you do this for all your neighbors?" he asks, bemused. "Is the entire block going to gain ten pounds because of your desserts?"

I blush because he's the only one I do this for consistently. Feeding him is just so rewarding. His enjoyment is palpable. "I like to be friendly with the people around me. It makes me feel like part of the community."

He cocks a brow and crosses his muscular arms over his chest while I lift the lid from the container and find plates to dish the apple pie onto. "So, you eat several desserts each night as you take them around to everyone?"

"No," I admit, refusing to look at him.

"Do you even know who your neighbor on the other side is?"

"Ethel." I glance up, pleased to see his surprise. "She and

I have had tea a couple of times." I find a spoon in one of his drawers and hand him the pie. "Are you finished questioning my motives? I can take the pie home if you'd prefer."

"No." He snatches it away and carries it to the table. "That would be cruel and unusual after you've let me smell it." He sits, spoon poised above the dessert, and waits for me to join him. I can't help but smile. Despite his protests, he likes my company—I'm sure of it. I pull out the seat opposite, and he digs in, only pausing after a few mouthfuls to ask, "So how are the plans coming along?"

"They're great." I help myself to my own piece of pie, which is about half the size of his. "I've secured twenty stalls and a judge for the biggest pumpkin competition."

He winces.

"What?" I ask.

"You're going to want at least three judges so you can call them a panel. Otherwise, someone will accuse the judge of being biased."

"It's *that* serious?" I push the pie away, unnerved. "I thought it was all a bit of fun."

"It's supposed to be." He shovels more pie into his mouth, closes his eyes, and hums in pleasure. "But the contestants take it very seriously. Margaret Adams once poisoned Tyrone Autry's pumpkin patch, and last year Tyrone accused my sister, Julia, of purchasing her winning pumpkin from a farm outside of town to win fraudulently."

"Wow." My lips twitch at the corners, then break into a smile. "Pumpkins are a serious business. Got it. I'll find two more judges. God forbid anyone be accused of pumpkin fraud."

My comment draws a reluctant chuckle. "Same goes for the apple pie contest. You want at least three tasters, and they can't be friends or else they might all support the same person regardless of who actually has the best pie."

"I appreciate the warning." It seems like there are more intricacies to consider than I'd imagined, but I'm not about to admit that when he's already made it clear he thinks it was a mistake for me to volunteer. I can do this.

Just like you can settle down in one place?

I shut down the voice in my mind. It wasn't not my fault things went south in the last place. Or the one before that.

Wyatt finishes his pie and eyes mine. "Oh, by the way, Sherry wants to know when you're free to do a reading at the library."

"Oh my gosh, I totally forgot! I can't believe it slipped my mind. Things have gotten crazy." Guilt slithers into my consciousness. I was so excited to talk to Sherry's book club, but the festival has occupied my thoughts all week. "I'll get in touch with her about it first thing tomorrow. Thanks so much for reminding me."

"No worries," he says, then gestures at my pie. "You going to eat that?"

I push it toward him, laughing. "Help yourself."

Wyatt

I PLACE the last lawn chair at the table just as Julia and Mom leave the house together, each carrying bowls of food and talking loudly.

"Oh, we're sitting here?" Julia asks, pausing as she spots the table and chairs in the shaded part of the lawn out the front of my house. "I'd rather be in the sun."

"Okay, birthday girl." I shift the table into a patch of

sunshine and then gather the chairs while she and Mom place their bowls down. Mom returns to the kitchen for more, and Julia starts setting out cutlery. We don't have fancy parties in our family. We prefer to keep celebrations low-key. Lunch on a Saturday fits the bill nicely. I even volunteered to host so Julia wouldn't have to clean up afterward. Although knowing her, she'll help anyway.

"How's the new neighbor?" she asks a little too casually.

"Fine." I keep my tone neutral. I'm not sure how much Mom has told her, but she's probably gotten a blow-by-blow of our relationship from the first meeting in the kitchen to me agreeing to show Felicity around town. Thank God no one has spilled the beans about our nightly dessert dates.

Not that they're dates.

Wrong word, bonehead.

"I heard you gave her the grand tour of Oak Bend." She collects three plates from a picnic bag on the ground and puts each in front of a chair. "Sources say you were smitten."

My jaw tightens. "Not funny, Jules."

She cocks her head, her curtain of brown hair spilling over her shoulders. "Come on, it kinda is."

"It'd be funnier if it were your love life they were messing with."

She grins. "I date just enough to keep Mom off my back. If you can't be bothered to do that, you have to be prepared for the consequences."

"This family" I mutter and stride inside to retrieve the cake I bought from the bakery earlier in the day. Once I've retrieved it from the pantry, I pause beside Mom, who slots a single candle into the center.

"Perfect." She pats my shoulder. "You've outdone yourself."

I roll my eyes. At least I know my limitations in the

kitchen, unlike Julia. I carry the cake out, and Mom follows with a bottle of wine and a can of beer. We each claim a seat, and Mom passes me the beer, then pours wine for herself and Julia.

"Happy birthday, sweetie," Mom says, her eyes crinkling at the corners. "You're officially in your late twenties now."

"I found my first gray hair this week," Julia replies, and I can't tell if she's joking or not. You can bet your ass she plucked that thing straight out of her head if she did find one. She may not admit it, but she's vain when it comes to her hair. "Let's eat."

I serve myself potato salad, and I'm about to shift a portion of bacon to my plate when a car pulls up at the curb and Felicity bounces out of it.

Julia cranes her neck to get a better look. "She's even prettier in person." She licks grease off her fingers. "Did I tell you I started reading one of her books?"

Felicity hasn't noticed us, but it won't be long before she does because she'll have to walk right past us to get to her front door. I watch her, recalling the way she looked at my dining table last night, sharing apple pie. Relaxed and beautiful but a little mussed, as though the day had ruffled her up. She's all put together now, with a knee-length pink skirt and white blouse that's tighter over her chest than around her waist because her tits are out of proportion to the rest of her. More than a handful, while she's petite. My mouth waters, and it doesn't want food.

"Someone looks *smitten*," Julia teases, voice low. "You should invite her over."

"No." I drag my gaze away from her and refocus on the bacon. "This is a family lunch."

"Don't be a spoilsport," Mom says. "We don't mind having her join us, do we, Jules?"

"Not at all."

Felicity starts up the drive, her laptop bag swinging at her side, and finally seems to notice us. She pauses, caught off guard, then waves brightly and continues toward her front door.

"Call her," Julia hisses.

I don't.

"Hi, Felicity!" my sister yells, and Felicity's head snaps around to look at us. "Come over here!"

A smile spreads over her face, lighting it up, and she changes direction and sashays across the lawn. "Hi." Her greeting is for the entire table. She turns to Julia. "I don't think we've met."

Julia stands and offers a hand. "I'm Julia. Wyatt's sister."

"So nice to meet you." She catches sight of the cake. "This looks like a family event. I don't want to intrude, so I'll see you another time."

"Stay," Julia insists.

"Yes, please do," Mom adds. "We'd love to get to know you better."

Felicity dithers, glancing at the cake again. "Are you sure?"

"Absolutely."

"Thank you." Her face lights up even more. "I'll grab another chair from the house."

Mom holds up a hand to stop her. "Never mind about that. Wyatt will get you one, won't you, dear?"

Grumbling, I get to my feet and march off to find another seat. We only have three lawn chairs, so I grab one from the dining table and bring it out, placing it between Mom and Julia to prevent them from pushing us together.

"I've been reading your book," Julia announces. "Chased by Darkness."

"Oh." Is it just me, or do Felicity's cheeks go pale? "Are you..." she swallows, "enjoying it?"

"So far, it's brilliant." Julia leans forward, radiating enthusiasm. "You're a talented writer."

"Thank you." Felicity's expression relaxes, but I can tell she's on edge. Her eyes dart around too quickly.

"Hey, are you okay?" I ask.

"Yeah." She lets out a shaky breath and tries to smile. "Sorry for overreacting. I get a bit defensive about my books because sometimes people are weird about them."

"Sweetheart." Mom waits until we all turn toward her. "There's nothing for you to be worried about."

"Thank you." This time her smile is genuine, if a bit tremulous.

Julia passes her the bottle of wine. "We can be a lot to handle. Feel free to drink this if it gets to be too much."

She laughs. "I won't need to do that. You've been nothing but kind and welcoming."

Mom and Julia share a glance.

"Just wait until they start the inquisition," I warn.

Right on cue, Mom asks, "Have you moved around a lot?"

Felicity blows out a sigh, stirring the curls by her cheek. "All my life. My mom was a serial dater, and every time she met a new man, we'd move."

"Sounds awful," Julia remarks, earning scowls from both Mom and me. "What? It does."

"It was," Felicity confirms. "I've moved around a few more places since college, but I want to find somewhere to settle down and call home. Oak Bend seems like a dream come true. I'm still waiting to wake up."

The last comment hits close to my heart. She wants to be here. To make a life for herself. But will she actually

60

stay? She's been away from her mom for years now and still hasn't settled. What makes her think this move will be any different?

Mom preens, as though she's single-handedly responsible for Felicity's good opinion of the town. "We're so glad you think so." She shares a look with Julia, who nods encouragingly. I bite back a groan. The matchmaking faeries are in full force. "We've been here our whole lives and never want to live anywhere else." She glances at me, her lips quirking. "In fact, Wyatt is more established than almost any other man you'll meet. All he needs is a good woman to make an honest man out of him."

Julia cackles. Felicity blushes. And enough is enough.

"Leave it alone," I growl, as if that will do any good where Mom is concerned.

But Felicity doesn't need me to rescue her. She stacks her dainty hands one on top of the other, smiles prettily, and throws her lot in with the rest of them. "Tell me all of Wyatt's most embarrassing stories." Her gaze slides over to mine and she winks. "Don't leave anything out."

Well, damn. Is she flirting?

I've never gotten the impression she's interested in me, except for the occasional instance when I've caught her checking me out, but that's just usual man-woman appreciation, isn't it? Or is it possible she'd like more?

Julia—loving sister that she is—hurries to bring out the big guns. In quick succession, Felicity hears about the time I broke my arm breakdancing in the bathroom while in junior high, the incident when I accidentally flashed my dick to the entire cheer squad, and most horrific of all, the day I called my teacher 'Mom.' My *male* teacher. At least she doesn't mention Dawn and Brody. I couldn't handle Felicity knowing about them yet. I like the way she looks at me as though I'm someone special and giggles into her hands while studying me from beneath her lashes. She treats me like I'm just a guy, and I never realized how much I miss that. The women around here either pussy-foot around me or think verbally lashing Dawn is the key to my heart. Felicity is a breath of fresh air, and if my heart hitches as I catch her smiling softly when she thinks I'm not looking—well, there's not much I can do about that.

CHAPTER 8

FELICITY

I LOVE WYATT'S FAMILY. They're exactly what I always wished I had. A mom who puts her children first. A sibling who likes to tease. And as for him? He's the caretaker, which is even more dangerous to my heart than his broody sexiness. He lets his guard down because he isn't worried they'll hurt him, and he isn't afraid to tease back. Best of all, any time anyone needs something, he's the first one there to help. Even if he mutters under his breath.

Now, as I stack dishes in his sink, I can hear laughter outside, and it fills me with joy. I run water and add a splash of detergent, humming to myself as I grab a dish brush and start scrubbing.

"You don't have to do that."

I jolt at the sound of Wyatt's voice, and turn to see him lingering in the doorway, one shoulder propped against the doorframe and his hands in his pockets.

"I want to," I tell him. "I gatecrashed Jules's birthday, so it's only fair."

He studies me with those inscrutable eyes. "You weren't gatecrashing. She invited you."

"Yes, that was lovely of her." I sigh, thinking again of the family I never had. The one I desperately want. "You're lucky to have them."

He straightens and crosses to my side. "I am. I know I can come across as ungrateful sometimes, but Mom and Jules are a blessing I'll never take for granted."

"Good," I whisper, trying not to tear up because he's so dang sweet. I lose the battle and sniffle. "They're special."

"Aw, hell," he says, seeing my watery eyes. "Come here." He steps closer and draws me into his arms. My eyes close, and I rest my head on his chest, enjoying the strength of his body and how safe he makes me feel.

"I can't tell what kind of tears these are," he mumbles, his lips moving against my temple. "Happy? Sad?"

"A bit of everything." I'm happy for what he's got, but I can't deny that I'm wallowing in self-pity too. He has what I've always wanted, and somehow that makes it seem even more out of reach. I pull away and force myself to smile, swiping at the moisture beneath my eyes. "I had the best time today, thank you."

He traces a finger around my hairline so gently the waterworks threaten to restart. "You don't have to be strong, you know." His expression is achingly tender, and my heart flips over. It almost looks like he cares about me, when all I've done is make myself at home in a life he never invited me to be part of. "It amazes me that you can be so upbeat given the childhood you had, but you don't have to be. You can be yourself with me."

I look down, studying the ground as my thoughts swirl wildly, because the alternative is to take his words the wrong way and make a fool of myself. He's being kind, and taking care of me, because that's what he does. It doesn't mean anything, does it?

"Hey, look at me."

I shake my head.

He places two fingers beneath my chin and gently tilts my face up. "I'm not great with words, and I know I'm not the easiest person to be around, but I'm here for you if you need me."

Oh, boy. My heart melts. It can't handle the sweet and swoony goodness that is Wyatt Dawson. Before I know it, I'm stretching onto my toes and brushing my lips against his. He stiffens the moment they touch, and I freeze.

What am I doing? This is a terrible idea. He's being friendly, not putting the moves on me. But then his gaze becomes intense, and he hauls me closer and sets his mouth over mine. His kiss is a claiming. It's just as blatant as everything else about him.

I want more.

I dig my fingers into his shoulders and hold him tight, the firm planes of his body uncompromising against the softness of mine. He kisses me like he wants it to go on forever—so do I, but his sister and mom are still outside. Not to mention that there's another woman in his life.

Oh, my God. I shove him away from me. I can't kiss him! Wyatt is tangled up with Dawn. I saw them having lunch together the other day.

"What?" he demands, breathing heavily.

My lip quivers. "Are you with Dawn?"

"No." His response is instantaneous and leaves no room for misinterpretation. "She's my ex."

Despite that, I sense him emotionally withdraw. The color leaches from his cheeks and he goes to the faucet and splashes water on his face.

"Fuck, what are we doing?"

"I don't know," I whisper, but based on the grooves of

pain and doubt etched onto his face, I'd say it's come to an abrupt halt.

"I'm sorry," he says, in a way that lets me know I won't like what's coming. "But I can't give you a relationship. That hasn't changed." He sighs. "This was a mistake."

"Oh." *Ouch.* I back away from him. "Got it. I'm sorry for starting this. I shouldn't have kissed you. I've got to go. I'll see you later." I spin on my heel and race out. *Coward.* His rejection is like being stabbed with an icicle after the wonderful day I've spent with his family, and I can't take it right now.

I'm so foolish. So naive.

He calls after me, but I don't stop, and I know he won't chase me in front of Nadine and Julia. I take the back exit to avoid them, rush to my place, and shut myself in my bedroom with my back to the door. Then I slide to the floor and bury my face in my palms. It's going to take a lot to save face after this.

I MANAGE to make it through the weekend without seeing Wyatt again. I don't take him dessert, opting to visit Ethel, my other neighbor, instead. She's a charming woman who's almost blind but makes the best sweet tea I've ever tasted. We talk about the festival, Oak Bend's history, and everything other than my mess of a life.

On Monday, I'm sitting at a table in Java by Jackie, working my way up to the climax of my story, when a sweet-faced old lady with a shock of vibrant pink hair approaches me.

"Hello, dear." She slides into the seat opposite me. "I'm

Marianne." She glances at my laptop, and her eyes light up. "Ooh, are you writing something?"

"I'm working on my next book," I reply. "It's nice to meet you." Even though I have no idea why she's joined me.

She waves at someone at a nearby table, then turns back to me. "I hear you've taken over the festival planning this year and wanted to make sure everything is on track."

"I think it is," I hedge, because while I've had a little guidance, I'm honestly not sure how I'm doing at this point.

She nods, her pink hair waving with the motion. "If you have people, attractions, and a permit, then you're all sorted."

"Permit?" My insides chill. "What permit?"

"Oh, no." Her face falls. "Did no one tell you?"

"Tell me what?" I ask, dread curdling in my stomach.

"Nothing can go ahead if you don't have a permit. The application needs to be submitted at least a month in advance to make sure it gets done on time." She cocks her head. "How long is it until the festival now?"

"Less than a month," I say, beginning to feel nauseous. "I didn't know. No one told me."

Marianne covers her mouth, looking as distressed as I feel. "But we can't miss the festival. We've had one every year for thirty-seven years."

Clenching my teeth together, I blink rapidly.

Don't cry. You can fix this.

But can I? Or am I doomed to screw it up the same way I do everything?

"Poor Christine probably forgot," Marianne continues, oblivious to my impending tears. "She has so much to do, and she juggles her responsibilities as well as she can, but sometimes something has to give."

"How..." I try to pull myself together because having a meltdown isn't going to solve anything. "How can I—"

"Excuse me," a voice breaks in from behind us.

We both turn. Sitting at the table to our rear is a handsome police officer with sandy brown hair and an easy smile.

"I couldn't help overhearing," he continues. "Am I right in thinking you haven't got the permit for the festival?"

"Um, yes," I admit.

Marianne's eyes narrow and she snaps, "We don't need your kind of help, Brody."

He holds his hands up in a placating gesture, his attention focused on me. "I have a cousin who works in the approvals office. I can talk to him and have the permit to you by the end of the day if you write the application now and give it to me at lunch time."

"Oh, my God, would you?" I ask, shoulders sagging in relief. "I'd never forgive myself if I screwed it up for everyone."

"It'll be fine," he assures me, his eyes warm. "I'll help you find the application form online, then all you need to do is fill it in and email it to me."

He drags his chair to us and leans over my laptop. Quickly, I exit out of the scene I was writing. I can't stand people looking at my work while it's in progress. It makes me jittery and uncomfortable.

"I don't think this is a good idea," Marianne hedges, her gaze darting between us. She wrings her hands, her lips forming a moue of disapproval. "Wyatt—"

"Isn't here and can't fix this," Brody interrupts smoothly.

I sneak a glance at him, wondering what's going on and what it has to do with Wyatt. Something is simmering beneath the surface, but as usual, I'm completely clueless.

That just feels par for the course these days. Besides, whatever it is, Brody's right that I need his help.

Marianne glances around the shop, then drops her voice and hisses, "People will talk."

"Let them."

I clear my throat. "So, can you show me how to find the form?"

"Of course." He takes the laptop from me, brings up a web browser, and a few moments later I'm staring at a fillable document, then he grabs a napkin and scrawls something on it with a pen from his pocket. He hands it to me. "This is my email address. Send me the application form as soon as you can, and I'll have my cousin fast-track it."

"Thank you," I whisper, tears of gratitude prickling my eyes.

"No problem." He shoves the chair back and stands. "I'd best leave you to it before Marianne gets any ideas about poisoning my coffee." He chuckles, but neither of us do the same. I really don't understand the dynamic here. Brody saunters to the front of the shop, waves at Ella, then leaves.

"What was that about?" I ask as soon as the door closes behind him.

"That no-good Brody Lang may look like Prince Charming, but don't let him fool you. Policeman or not, he's as slick and slimy as a snake oil salesman."

I shrug. "He seemed nice enough to me."

She laughs. "Of course he does. He's a practiced liar."

Wow. The animosity is real. I feel like I've been drawn into a family feud, only no one told me what started it or who's on each side.

"I'd better get to work on this application." I nod toward the computer. "I don't have much time."

Not taking the hint, she remains seated. "Don't let him trick you, Felicity. The man is trouble."

"I'll keep that in mind," I tell her.

She gets to her feet and wrings her hands again. "Be careful."

"Thanks for the warning."

"Bye now."

I wave as she goes, then concentrate on the task in front of me. Two hours later, I email the application to Brody Lang. Three hours after that, he asks me to meet him in the town square. When I arrive, I scan the area and spot him standing on the steps outside a stone building. He holds up a sheet of paper. As I draw close, I can read "Granted" stamped across front in blocky red letters.

"All done," he says, grinning as if he's just got down from his white horse. I half expect him to bow gallantly as he hands it over.

"Thank you so much!" Overwhelmed by relief, I throw my arms around him.

CHAPTER 9

WYATT

I'M PASSING through the town square in search of an afternoon snack when I witness something that both chills my blood and sets it alight.

Felicity, in Brody Lang's arms.

My heart—that stupid lump of coal in my chest—thumps painfully, and my mind superimposes an image over the one in front of me, of Brody Lang, balls-deep in Dawn. In my bed. Except the image blurs, replacing Dawn's face with Felicity's. I shake my head, desperate to dispel the awful vision.

Felicity steps back, beaming up at Brody, with papers clutched in her hand. Meanwhile, I fight the urge to slink away to a dark corner and hide. I didn't realize they knew each other, but I suppose I should have expected Brody to move in on her as soon as he heard she existed. It's hard to believe the jackass and I used to be friends. Still, even though I hate drama, I can't sit back and let the image of him with Felicity come true. I just can't. Perhaps I haven't wanted to admit it—and okay, I've been a bit of a dick—but Felicity is mine, and I'm not going to let him take her.

A few strides carry me to them, and then I slide my arms around Felicity, drawing her close, and kissing her full on the mouth. She squeaks in surprise, but her body softens against me the same way it did in my kitchen. She hums in the back of her throat and gives me her weight, trusting me to support her. I'll make myself worthy of that trust. My tongue delves into her mouth, partly because I can't help myself and partly because I want to make sure Brody knows how totally uninterested she is in him. She sighs, welcoming me. She tastes faintly of coffee and something sweet. Felicity probably always tastes sweet. It's her essence.

Her hands go to my chest and smooth over it, as though she's soothing a giant beast. I want to lean into her touch and purr, but damned if I'm going to let Brody see how lost I am over her. I pull back, separating our lips, then press a kiss to her forehead, securing her against me with one arm.

"I see you've met the honorable Officer Lang." I imbue the word 'honorable' with every bit of disdain I have for him, which is a significant amount.

Felicity blinks owlishly. "Yes, he fixed a permit problem for me."

I glance at Brody suspiciously. I should be the one to fix her problems. Not Officer Asshat.

"That's all it was," he assures me, palms out in a gesture of peace. "She was thanking me because of something that got overlooked for the Fall Harvest and Crafts Festival."

I look down at her, determined not to let her see how riled I am. I'd hate to unnerve her. Especially when it's a miracle she hasn't shoved me away yet. I'm blowing hot and cold, and she deserves better than that.

"Why didn't you ask me for help?"

She shrugs one shoulder. "Brody was there when I found out. He leapt to my rescue."

"I'll just bet he did," I mutter, wondering how much trouble I'd get into for threatening a police officer.

She gives me a strange look, clearly bewildered as to what's going on, which means no one has enlightened her about my relationship history. Something to be grateful for. At least she hasn't questioned me in front of Brody or removed my body from hers. I'm draped all over her and considering how we parted, she must be confused as hell.

"You know me," Brody murmurs. "I love to help the ladies."

My fingers flex into Felicity's shoulder. I know what his version of 'help' entails.

"Felicity is new to town," I tell him, even though this is something he probably knows. "We've been seeing each other." I notice one of her eyebrows furrow, and I plead with my eyes for her not to say anything.

"Good for you." Brody's hands go to his hips, and his smirk suggests he's about to open a can of worms. "I was afraid you'd let what happened with Dawn get into your head and stop you from moving on."

"Fuck off."

Felicity gasps. "Wyatt!"

I keep her tucked against my side and meet her eyes, ignoring our audience. "You don't know the whole story. I'll tell you later."

She nibbles on her lip, visibly torn, but nods, choosing to trust me, and damned if that doesn't feel good. "Thanks for your help, Brody," she says. "But Wyatt and I are overdue for a coffee date. See you later."

He nods to her. "Take care, darling, and don't believe everything you hear about me."

"Don't worry." Her eyes glint with a steeliness I never expected to see in them. "I make up my own mind. I'll see you around." With that, she takes my arm and drags me away from him. I send a parting glare, then let myself be moved because Felicity wants to talk, and at this point I'd say that's the least she deserves.

Felicity

WHY ARE men so freaking confusing?

Wyatt is acting like a jealous boyfriend, and I have no idea why. But I intend to find out. There's obviously some kind of negative energy between him and Brody. And what was with that kiss? He practically blew me off after we kissed the other day, and now here he is, laying one on me for all and sundry to see in the middle of the town square. He's a complicated man, and right now, I just don't get him.

I lead him around the corner, out of sight of the square, and spot his truck a block or so away. We walk in silence until we reach it, and then he exhales slowly, the tension shuddering out of his big body.

"What was that about?" I ask, leaning on his passenger door.

He gets into the driver's seat and gestures for me to climb in. I do, even though being in a confined space with him seems like the worst idea ever when my entire body is still thrumming from his kiss. My nerves are on high alert, my hormones singing with glee.

He reaches across the space between us and takes my hand. His palm is rough and callused, and the friction of it sends a delicious shiver racing through me. "Come home and I'll make you a coffee while I explain."

"Okay." I have everything I need with me, and I'm not operating on a particular schedule.

He relaxes again, and I wonder how wound-tight he's been. He drives us to his place and parks out front, then I follow him inside and wait at the table while he prepares two mugs of coffee. It feels oddly domestic. Once we're sitting opposite each other, he fidgets. I wait patiently, not wanting to push him. Something is bothering him—something big—and I'm not used to being the person anyone wants to confide in, so I'm not going to do anything to ruin it.

"Can I touch you?" he asks eventually. "It calms me."

I melt a little. "Uh, sure."

Big, gruff, broody guy likes to touch? I'm down for that.

"Let's go to the sofa," he says, and strides into the living room, leaving his mug behind. I follow and snuggle against him. His arm falls around my shoulder as though it's the most natural thing ever, and it strikes me again how strange this all is. A complete 180 from 'I don't do relationships.'

"So?"

"So." He drops his hand to my waist and pulls me closer, but his gaze is out the window, unfocused. "You've met Dawn?"

"Yeah." I don't expand on this because it's his turn to talk.

"We dated for two years," he says. "It ended six months ago when I came home early one evening and found her having sex with Brody in our bed."

Oh, wow.

My gut drops, and I don't reply. I mean, what is there to say? I can't imagine what he went through. Seeing his girlfriend's betrayal firsthand must have devastated him.

"I'm so sorry. That's awful."

He continues staring out the window but blinks a few times and my heart goes 'aww.' Leaning over, I kiss his jaw. His sexy, square jaw that's much more attractive than Brody's clean cut one. Wyatt is more appealing than Brody, full stop.

"I can't believe anyone would cheat on you." My temper starts to rise, heating my cheeks and burning in my chest. "Dawn is an idiot. You are gold, Wyatt. Pure gold. And she's a... Well, she doesn't deserve you—or your pain."

"Thanks." The edge of his mouth softens, and he glances at me. "I'm gold, huh?"

"Yes." I nod firmly. "You should know that nothing happened between Brody and me. I literally just met him, and I have no desire to get to know him better." Feeling the need to make sure he unequivocally knows what kind of person I am, I add, "If you and I were together, I would never, ever touch another man. You'd be all the man I'd need."

CHAPTER 10

WYATT

YOU'D BE ALL the man I'd need.

Yeah, I can't un-hear that. My insides are all over the place, twisted in dozens of tight knots, and I feel like she's picking at the edges of them, loosening the threads.

"I'd like you to be mine," I admit, taking a plunge off a metaphorical cliff and hoping she'll be there to catch me at the bottom. "But I have a hard time trusting, and I might get jealous or possessive."

She angles her face toward mine, smiling sweetly. "I can live with that. But—"

Uh oh, I don't like the sound of that.

"—you need to *try* to trust me. I don't mind a little jealousy, and I'm happy to be transparent with you about what's going on in my life, but if I feel like you're waiting for me to let you down, I'm not sure I can handle that."

"I'll try," my mouth agrees before my brain can catch up. She beams, and a flash of premonition chills me because I might be making a terrible mistake. I may have told her the truth about how my relationship failed, but I left out important details, like the part where Dawn yelled hateful things at me and blamed me for driving her into Brody's arms by being stingy with affection. She called me cold. Emotionally distant. Stunted. And hell, maybe she was right, because I just turned around and walked away. The next day, I ordered her to remove her things from my home, not even flinching when she cried and begged me to reconsider. I don't want Felicity to see me the way Dawn did. If history were to repeat itself, I couldn't make it through to the other side.

But maybe it won't, the little voice in the back of my mind whispers. *Maybe Felicity's unstable upbringing means she doesn't have the same expectations as Dawn.*

As soon as I think it, I feel sick. I don't want Felicity to settle for less than she deserves. I want to be the man she thinks she sees when she looks at me. She's still smiling now, even though I've been weirdly silent. Does she realize what a gift she's giving me?

Without thinking, I kiss her. Her lips part on a gasp, and I wish I could be slow and gentle, but this kiss is a claiming. I need to know she's mine. I need to brand her somehow. To make it so she can't possibly change her mind. I deepen the kiss, and she rides along with me, accepting me, letting me take control. She's so precious. I should be holding her like she's spun glass, but instead, I drag her onto my lap and practically maul her. She utters a contented sigh and nestles over my erection. I groan deep in my throat. Thank God she's not the type to be scandalized by an errant hard-on.

"Sorry," I mutter. "I just..."

"Don't be." She rests her head on my shoulder. "I love it when you do that." She glances at the clock on the wall. "Shouldn't you be working?"

"Yeah." But I don't want to let her go.

"Why don't you head back, and as soon as you're done,

come over and we can have apple crumble," she suggests. "I made some earlier."

I chuckle. "Do you ever actually write, or do you spend all of your time baking?"

"I write plenty," she says tartly. "But a girl needs fuel, too."

Secretly, I think she bakes because she knows how much I love it, and it gives her an excuse to spend time with me. I would never suggest that to her face, though, because if I embarrassed her, she might stop, which is the last thing I want.

"Fair enough." I kiss her temple, lingering there, breathing her in. Her hair smells fruity—perhaps of peaches —and it's really fucking nice. "You're right. I should go, but I'll be back in a couple of hours."

She nods, and climbs off me. I bite back the urge to ask her to stay right here on my couch and not move. That wouldn't be fair, however much I might like the thought of it.

We walk outside together, and she goes to her place while I return to my truck. The rest of the afternoon passes slowly, as though the prospect of seeing her again makes everything drag out. When I finally finish, I give myself a cursory sniff—not too bad—and go to her without showering because I'm that eager to see her.

I knock, feeling strangely hesitant because she's usually the one to approach me, but there's no need for nerves because as soon as she throws open the door, she wraps me in a hug. My arms close around her and tension I hadn't even realized existed eases from my body.

"I missed you," I tell her.

She giggles. "It's been two hours."

"Don't care." I press my lips to her forehead. "It was too long."

She grins so widely her face threatens to split, and I adore it. She's happy because of me. That's a heady feeling. She stretches up and kisses me. It's chaste and over too soon, but it hits me like one of Mom's smacks upside the head.

Thwack. All the feels.

I rub my hand to my chest, uncomfortable with the emotions burning there.

"Come in," she says, inviting me inside her home. It shouldn't mean so much when I've been inside the place dozens of times over the years Mom has owned it, but she's letting me into her sanctuary, and that's important. We pass down the hall and into a living room that doesn't look much different from when the place was empty.

Huh.

My brows draw together. Where's the essence of Felicity? The bright colors and cheerful decor?

She continues into the kitchen, which is similarly bare, and opens the fridge, drawing out a tray of crumble. She grabs a pair of bowls and serves one for each of us.

"You haven't unpacked much," I remark. "Do you need a hand? I'm happy to help."

She reaches into the freezer and grabs a tub of ice cream. "I'm fully unpacked, but thanks for the offer." She glances up and must catch my expression because she adds, "I don't own a lot because I've moved around so much, but I'm planning to change that. I'm thinking maybe I need a plant for the counter and another for my desk."

"Plants are a serious commitment." My lips twitch with amusement as I recall the way she attacked her garden, clearly unable to differentiate flowers from weeds. "Think you can handle it?"

She pivots to face me. "I am *beyond* ready."

I grab her by the hips and kiss the tip of her nose because she's so damn irresistible.

A flush crawls up her cheeks. "How much ice cream do you want?"

"None." I swipe one of the plates, put it in the microwave, and then help myself to a spoon from her drawer. "Don't like ice cream."

Her jaw drops. "Please say you're joking."

I shake my head.

"Oh, my God." She pinches the bridge of her nose and closes her eyes for a brief moment. "Let me get this straight. You have a sweet tooth and love nearly every type of dessert *except* ice cream?"

"Yeah." I nod, confirming her statement.

"But... but..." Her mouth opens and closes. "Ice cream is delicious. Everyone loves it." She slides the tub off the counter and holds it up. "How can you not love triple chocolate fudge with salted caramel?"

I shrug. "Just don't."

She sets the tub down and swats my chest. "You're a monster. Inhuman. There's something wrong with you."

"You're only just figuring that out?" I remove my crumble from the microwave and replace it with hers.

"This might be a deal-breaker," she mutters.

Taking her by the shoulders, I sweep her into a kiss that seems to last forever, so she won't forget the perks of being with me.

She blinks, dazed. "Not a deal-breaker."

My lips quirk. "Good."

Felicity

PETER'S LEGS *burned as he sprinted along the corridor, taking a sharp left into a chamber he hadn't yet entered and praying to whatever deity may be listening for deliverance. He put his back to the door, trying to calm his breathing. Footsteps clacked along the concrete floor, and then—*

"Excuse me, Felicity, do you have a moment to talk?"

I flinch, my hand flying to my chest, breath catching in my throat. "Marianne, you frightened me!"

The old woman's face pales, her expression contrite. "Sorry, dear."

"No, it's okay." Raking my hair back from my face, I inhale slowly. "I was caught up in the scene, that's all."

"I could see that." She takes the seat opposite me at the table I've come to think of as mine, in the back of Java by Jackie. "Don't worry, this won't take a minute."

"Okay." I sit back, my heart still racing. "What's up?"

"You were seen kissing Wyatt yesterday in public, immediately after hugging that scoundrel Brody Lang. Is there mischief afoot?"

"Not at all," I promise. "I was thanking Brody for helping me. As for Wyatt," I blush, "He and I are seeing each other, but it's nothing serious yet."

"I'm so glad to hear that." She breaks into a smile. "He deserves something good in his life."

"I think so too," I agree.

"Well." She stands. "I'll leave you to," she waves a hand, "whatever *that* is. Take care, love."

"Bye." I watch her go and then try to climb back inside Peter and his fear.

A few hours later, I flop onto my sofa, extending my legs out ahead of me. My eyes wander through the window to the house next door. I wonder if Wyatt is home. Should I invite myself over? I've been doing so nearly every day under the guise of bringing dessert, but I got so wrapped up in my story that I haven't baked anything today. Are we at the point in our relationship where it's expected that I'll come over, or should I give him space?

I'm saved from my own thoughts by a knock. Getting to my feet, I teeter as my head spins from moving too quickly, then right myself. At the door, I pause and check the peephole. Holy hotness. Turning the handle, I yank it inward, and the breath whooshes from my chest at the mouthwatering sight of Wyatt Dawson on my doorstep, his brawny arms exposed for the world to see, bearing bags from the local bakery.

"Oh, wow." My gaze zips from him to the bags and back again, unsure which I'm more pleased to see. Finally, I settle on him. "Isn't it my job to turn up uninvited with baked goods?"

"I'm officially giving you the night off." He offers me the bags, and I take them. "Can I come in?"

"Sure." Like a dolt, I realize I'm blocking the way. I hurry to move, and humor gleams in his eyes. "You, uh, smell good."

He smells good? I mentally slap my forehead. Shut up, Felicity.

"It's probably the donuts."

I fist pump. "I knew I could smell donuts. Are they chocolate? Custard? Is there cream?"

"Look for yourself."

Peeking inside the first bag, I almost moan at the sight of a cream-filled donut with chocolate frosting. "Please tell me this is mine."

"All yours."

One side of his mouth hitches up, making him almost as delectable as the donut. We sit on the sofa, and he wraps one of his arms around me, securing me to his side while he grabs a caramel-glazed donut with the other. We eat in silence. He finishes before me, then watches me with an intensity that makes my cheeks flame. When I lick my fingers and his jaw tightens, I can't resist kissing him. He drags me onto his lap, and I sigh happily because it feels like I'm surrounded by a wall of muscle on all sides. The kiss continues until I pull away to catch my breath.

"Do you have any idea what you do to me?" he murmurs, more than heat shining in his eyes. There's vulnerability too. I can see how difficult it is for him to let it show, but he's trying, and that means everything.

"About the same thing you do to me," I confess, making sure he knows he's not alone.

He nuzzles the juncture of my neck and shoulder, and I shiver and clutch him tighter. "Tell me about yourself."

I laugh breathlessly. "You already know the good parts."

His lips touch my skin, and I angle my head so he can trace them up the side of my neck to my hairline. He threads his fingers through my hair and rubs circles on my temples with his thumbs. I go limp in his arms. Feels. So. *Good*.

"How'd you end up in Oak Bend?" he asks.

Ugh. This isn't a story I want to share, but he's venturing outside his comfort zone for me and the least I can do is return the favor.

"I needed to leave the place I was living before here. They, uh, found out what I write, and suddenly, all my friends weren't friends anymore. They stopped talking to me. Gossiped about me behind my back." My throat tightens, and it's all I can do to bite out the last few words. "They made out like I was a monster."

"Aw, baby, no." He kisses the tip of my nose. "You have an imagination, that's all."

"Thanks." Sometimes I struggle to believe that myself. Don't get me wrong, I know I'm not a monster, but maybe my mind is a little more twisted than most. "Anyway, I searched for rentals online, saw this one and liked the look of it, so here I am."

"Well, I can promise that you won't be turned into an outcast in Oak Bend. We take care of people, whatever their quirks."

I smile despite myself. "I'm beginning to see that."

We sit in silence for a couple of minutes, and I rest my head on his shoulder. Just as I'm about to suggest we eat a proper meal, Wyatt speaks again.

"Don't take this the wrong way..."

Uh oh. Nothing good ever starts with that phrase.

"But is your default to run when things get hard?"

What the...?

My jaw drops, and I squirm off his lap. Suddenly, I don't want to cuddle. Is he suggesting I'm a coward who should have stayed and faced the disdain and rejection I left behind?

"Whoa," he grumbles, grabbing at my hand and holding on when I try to shake him off. "I'm not judging you. Just asking. Is that your way of handling things?"

"No," I protest, hating that he's touching me so sweetly while accusing me of things that have me bristling. But the more I think about it and acknowledge the fact that I've kept moving ever since college ended, even when there was no Mom to drag me around, the more I begin to wonder. I had reasons for leaving each place—reasons that seemed rock

85

solid at the time—but I have to admit, I do tend to run away. Sure, nobody could argue I should have stayed in a hostile environment, but not all of the towns and cities I've lived in were hostile. Many were nice enough, but in some cases, I had relationships that fell apart and staying seemed awkward. And other times, I had this certainty that something better was around the next bend in the road.

My hand goes to my mouth, and I whimper.

"Felicity?" he asks. "You okay?"

"I do," I whisper to him, horrified. "I do run."

He kisses the back of my hand and bundles me into his arms. I don't fight this time, just let him hold me. With the massive realization I had, I need all the comfort I can get. Has it been my fault all this time that I've never found a place to belong? Is it my itchy feet and unwillingness to deal with discomfort that's the reason everything I own fits in my car?

"Don't run from me." His voice is soft and pleading. "Promise me. Even if I'm a jerk at times, don't run."

"I promise." I tilt my face up to his, needing a distraction. Needing to taste his desire and be reminded of his solidity. Our lips meet in an explosion of emotion, as though we've each lowered our floodgates and everything we've kept inside for so long is rushing out. A tsunami of feelings.

Within seconds, I'm being cradled against his chest as he carries me from the sofa into the bedroom. Gently, he lowers me to the bed and descends on top of me, pressing me into the mattress, his body a delicious weight against mine. His erection is firm against the bud of nerves between my legs that are crying out for him to hurry up and get me naked. I tug his face down to mine and kiss him again, hating the interruption for even a few seconds. We lie there, me pinned beneath him and enjoying every minute of it.

Our breathing grows more labored, and my limbs slowly melt into mindless languor. But then, he rolls off me with a regretful sigh and stares at the ceiling.

"Why are you stopping?" I ask, ready to climb on top of him and demand more.

He reaches blindly behind himself, grabs a pillow, and growls into it. When he tosses it aside, he turns to meet my questioning gaze. "We can't get too carried away. I want to give you time to get used to the idea of us together."

I groan, my heated body beginning to cool. "Fine."

He has a point, but why does he have to be so damned concerned with my state of mind when I'd gladly throw caution to the wind?

CHAPTER 11

WYATT

In the week that follows, I take Felicity out to eat at the diner a couple of times, and on another night, she makes me a home-cooked meal to rival Mom's. We get our hands on each other at every opportunity and make out like teenagers, but we never go further. I enjoy being with her. She's fun and makes me smile more than I can recall doing in years. In fact, I feel like a goof every time I hear her footsteps coming up the path. But I'm sick of holding back. I want more from her than kisses, and I think she might finally be ready, too. I've been careful not to rush her, but every time we go our separate ways, she seems to grow more frustrated, which means one thing: tonight is the night.

It's Friday, and somehow, she's convinced me to attend karaoke at Bender's Bar. I've been before—usually with Julia, who loves getting on stage even though she's tone deaf —but I've never sung myself. I have a feeling that's about to change. Felicity isn't the kind of woman to take a back seat, and she won't let me do so either. That's one of the things I like about her. She sees me and doesn't let my gruffness dissuade her. She just smiles, kisses me, and does what she wanted to from the beginning.

When I get home from work, covered in dust and sweat, I shower briefly and dress in jeans and a t-shirt. Bender's isn't one of those places where you need to go the extra mile. As soon as Felicity arrives, I feel under-dressed. She breezes into the living room wearing a lilac dress that stops halfway down her thighs and has the kind of floaty skirt that would be so damn easy to slip my hand underneath to discover what panties she's wearing. Her hair falls in sexy waves around her shoulders, and her lips are petal pink. One of my arms snags her waist, and I sweep her close for a kiss. She giggles, her hands resting on my chest. There's something about the way she does that, with her small palms sitting over my heart, that make me want to roar like King Kong.

"You look beautiful," I tell her.

She glances down, and a wrinkle forms between her brows. "Is it too much?"

"Not at all." She can dress however she damn well likes. I don't care if she looks better than anyone else there, although I might have to fend off unwanted advances. Every guy in town is going to be crazy with lust once they see her like this. I kiss her again and touch my forehead to hers. "Never seen anything so pretty."

She smiles. Not a big one that lights up her face, but a small, shy one that comes right from her heart. "Thanks. I forgot I had it until I moved here, and it's too nice to leave in the closet." She lays her hand on my arm. "Shall we go?"

I usher her outside, into my truck. I don't intend to drink anything stronger than a root beer, so I'll be safe to drive her home later. If we get naked, I want to have control of all my faculties so there's no chance of her being disappointed.

"What should I expect?" she asks as she buckles her seatbelt.

"Drunk old men, a few women Mom's age, and whatever unlucky guys want to catch the game tonight."

I glance over. She's nibbling on her lip, looking thoughtful. "Do they sing well? Because I'm not exactly Rihanna."

A chuckle rumbles from deep inside me. "How well do you think Jimmy the builder sings when he's four beers in?"

She nods. "Point made. Sorry for worrying."

"Hey." I lean over and kiss her cheek. "What happened to the Felicity who couldn't wait to belt out Shania Twain at the top of her lungs?"

"Okay, okay." She laughs. "I'm being silly. I don't know why. I'm excited, I just..." She doesn't finish the sentence, but I know what she means. She wants to fit in. To belong. And she's worried she won't. I can understand her fears, but everyone loves her, and it's about time she realized it.

I drive us to the bar and park outside, along with a dozen or so other vehicles. We head in and pause in the doorway while our eyes adjust to the dim lighting. A space has been cleared at the end of the room opposite the bar, and two women in their forties occupy the makeshift stage, performing a duet. It takes me a few moments to recognize the song as Bon Jovi's *You Give Love a Bad Name* because their rendition is that terrible. Beside me, Felicity relaxes.

"Thank God," she mutters, then claps a hand over her mouth and peeks at me as though she didn't mean to speak out loud.

I smother a laugh. "Come on, baby. Let's find a seat." I take her hand in mine, and we wind between the tables to a spot in the corner. I rest my back against the wall and draw her to my chest, both of us facing the show. Her hair tickles my chin, and I brush my lips against the top of her head. She's all softness in my arms, letting me hold her as though she doesn't care who sees. My heart swells with affection as she rests her forearms over my own and clutches me to her. Dawn would never have let me be all over her like this in public. She preferred to keep the PDA to a minimum and flirt indiscriminately. At the time, I didn't think much of it. That was just how she was. But in hindsight, it probably should have been a red flag.

The women finish their song and hand the microphone over to an older gentleman named Duane, who used to own a farm on the outskirts of town. He retired a few years ago and took up country-western singing to pass the days. The music for *The Gambler* by Kenny Rogers starts up, and he leaps in flawlessly.

"Wow," Felicity breathes. "Glad we didn't walk in when he was singing, or I'd have major stage fright." She leans back and tilts her face up to look at me. "How do we sign up?"

I gesture to a book on the table nearest the stage. "People write their name and song of choice. There are a few hundred options recorded, but they can find most anything on YouTube."

"Perfect." She separates herself from me and beelines for the book. I consider whether to follow, but she seems to have everything in hand, so I wait until she returns, enjoying the flush on her cheeks. "I'm next."

"Can I get you a drink?" I ask, knowing that alcohol helps me release my inhibitions and might do the same for her.

"Wine?" she asks.

"No problem." I head to the bar, nodding to the guy

behind it. He's not someone I recognize. Several years younger than me—probably not long out of school. "Can I get the house wine and a root beer?"

He serves up one of each, but I've only made it halfway back when Duane's song finishes, and Felicity practically skips across the floor to the stage to takes the microphone. Duane winks at her—the old flirt—and says something, probably offering to sing backup, but she shakes her head and rolls back onto her heels as the music switches over. When I hear what she's chosen, I have to laugh.

"Let's go girls," she sings. "C'mon."

Yeah, she's about as good at singing as she thought she was. Not bad enough to make anyone cover their ears, but certainly not good enough for anyone to *want* to listen to her. Except... there's something charming about her enthusiasm as she jumps into *Man! I Feel Like a Woman!*

She's too fucking cute.

My fingers curl into my palms, and I glance around the patrons to see if anyone looks anything other than complimentary. If so, I'll introduce them to the exit. Or my fist. But they all seem as entertained by her as I am, bobbing their heads along to the beat. She jumps around and dances terribly as the chorus hits. Someone whoops, and I want to high-five them. When she finishes, a smattering of applause breaks out. She points at me and beckons. I frown and shake my head.

She speaks into the microphone. "Wyatt, the next one is a duet."

Oh, hell, no.

I groan, but she's so eager I'm not sure I can turn her down.

"I'll sing with you, sweetheart," some asshat calls. I shoot him a glare and bust my ass over to her side.

Felicity

WYATT LOOKS like he wants to be up here in front of everyone about as much as he wants a kick in the nuts, but he joins me anyway, and that makes my spirit soar. Ever since I watched *High School Musical* as a teenager, I've loved what duets symbolize—the togetherness of them—but I never thought I'd find someone to sing with me. When the opportunity arose, I couldn't turn it down. Hopefully, he's not too mad. I give him a hesitant smile, and his gaze softens, becoming less murderous. I love the way it transforms when he looks at me.

The opening strains of the song begin, and he glances at the lyric screen to see what I chose. I'm not sure how much he'll read into it, or how much I actually want him to. His eyes lock on me and don't waver as he sings the first verse of *Don't Go Breaking My Heart* by Elton John. His gaze holds as much meaning as the lyrics, and it's intense enough for a shiver to ripple down my spine. When my part begins, I have to look away to read the words, but as soon as I've memorized them, I return to staring at him. He's gorgeous. Big and strong. His voice is surprisingly mellow, and I like it. Perhaps it's not what you'd think of as classically good, but it's deep and raspy and makes me think all manner of things I have no right to.

Like love.

Like forever.

I know we're just taking this a day at a time, but I've never felt so strongly about a man before. We fit. His weird and my weird are aligned.

I put my whole heart into the song, even as I try to keep

it light and playful so we don't freak out the audience. When we finish, Wyatt grabs my hand and drags me outside. A hearty cheer follows us through the side exit into an alley. The moment the door closes, he pins me to the wall and kisses me. He steals my breath. I sway into him and thank my lucky stars he's solid enough that his balance doesn't waver.

"Is that enough karaoke?" he asks, drawing back.

My mind is flooded by hormones, and I struggle to understand him. "Uh, yeah."

"Great. Can I take you home?"

"Sure," I answer absent-mindedly, then jerk to reality as he starts to usher me out of the alley. "Wait. My place. Let's go to my place."

He grunts to indicate he heard but doesn't use words. We drive in near silence. My hand wanders up the inside of his thigh, and he groans.

"Hands to yourself, or I'll be forced to stop."

Disappointed, I withdraw and intertwine my fingers in front of me so they don't return to him without my permission. He parks in his driveway, and we detour over to my place. I unlock the door but fumble with the key when he comes up behind me and sets his lips on the back of my neck.

"Oh, God." I shiver. "You're distracting me."

"Good." He reaches around me and gently takes the key, slotting it into the door while I lean back into him and kiss his cheek. He shoves the door open and urges me into the hall—my knees are too weak to do anything other than comply. He escorts me to my bedroom, then freezes in the doorway.

I glance around, momentarily forgetting what must have distracted him, but then I remember what I did before leaving. I had to make sure this night ended the way I wanted, so two small lamps frame the bed, casting a romantic glow around the room. Music plays from the sound system. Something jazzy, without lyrics. A pink silk cover is spread across the bed, because for some reason I thought it might look sexy.

Wyatt turns to me and raises a brow. "Is this a seduction?"

I squirm, my cheeks blazing. "Uh, guilty."

His lips curve into a slow smile that melts me in all the best places. "Smart. I was just going to rely on my charm."

"You wanted to seduce me tonight?"

"Yeah," he admits. "Seems like we both had the same idea."

Taking his hand, I lead him to the bed, but when we reach it, he sweeps me off my feet and deposits me on the center of the mattress. Giggling, I part my thighs and he crawls between them and settles in. He cups my face with his palm and mesmerizes me with his beautiful brown eyes.

"You're gorgeous," he murmurs, then presses his lips to mine.

My mouth softens beneath his, and when his fingers firm on my chin and I gasp, his tongue delves inside, tasting me. My body reacts, nipples puckering, heat pooling at my core and coalescing as he rocks forward, creating friction in the most delicious ways. Sighing, I lie back and enjoy his kisses as they journey across my cheek, down my neck, and reach the neckline of my dress. I tug at it, trying to get it out of the way, but he stills me with a hand.

"Take it easy. I love this dress. Want to see you in it again. That can't happen if you tear it."

I raise my arms and shimmy out of it, with his assistance. Wyatt hovers above me, staring at me as though I truly am dessert. I love it. No one has ever looked at me this way before. He lowers himself down and brushes his lips over my navel, his scruff delightfully scratchy against my soft stomach. His whiskers tickle as they traverse my body.

He scoots down the bed and kisses the inside of my calf. I whimper. Who knew the leg was an erogenous zone? His gaze flicks up to my face, then returns to the flesh in front of him. His lips find the back of my knee, then my inner thigh. My back arches, offering my pussy to him shamelessly. I've never done that with a man, and I'm certain I'm blushing everywhere. Considering my mother's never-ending quest for love and the man-chasing environment in which I was raised, I'm remarkably innocent. I mean, I've had sex. Of course I have. I'm at the dark end of my twenties. But it's been incredibly vanilla, and no one has ever gone down on me.

That changes the instant Wyatt Dawson lays his sinful mouth over my panties and licks me through the fabric. My hips jerk, the sensation far more intense than I expect. His muscular forearms land one on either side of his head, holding my thighs down as they buck, desperate to either escape or wrap around him and not let go.

"Oh, God," I rasp, my brain hardly able to function as he makes my pleasure his personal mission. He pulls my panties to the side and slicks his tongue between my folds. My fingers clench the silk bedspread, and my head tilts back as my eyes close.

"Shh," he murmurs against me. "Just let go. I've got you."

He does, too. I'm not sure he even realizes how much he has me.

As he licks and sucks and tastes, sounds of his enjoyment echo in the back of his throat, turning me on, making me even wetter. When his tongue flicks my clit, I cry out.

A PLACE TO BELONG

"Please, Wyatt. Please, please, please." I don't even know what I'm begging for. Mercy, maybe. For him to either finish me off or let me go. What I get is a vicious curse as I crane my neck to look at him and he meets my eyes.

He pulls back, panting, and licks his lips. "You taste as sweet as you are." He places a tender kiss on my belly, resting his cheek there. "I have no fucking clue why you want me out of all the men in this town when all I've done is try to push you away, but thank you. For sharing your sweetness with me."

Holy crap. I'm a puddle of hormones, hovering on the brink of orgasm, and he goes and says something like that?

"I'll always choose you," I whisper, hoping he can see how much I mean it. "You're a good man, and I—" I can't tell him I love him. Not like this. "I want you to make love to me," I finish instead.

"Yes." He lifts himself onto his forearms, rolls off the bed, and digs in his wallet for a condom. He rolls it on, then pauses before returning to me. "You're sure?"

"One hundred percent. I want you and only you."

He blinks rapidly, and if I didn't know better, I'd think he were on the verge of tearing up, but then he lands on top of me and slides the first inch of his erection inside. Instantly, I forget everything I've ever known.

"More," I insist, greedy for him.

He thrusts forward, filling me up. I gasp and toss my head back.

"Fuck, you're sexy," he rasps and repeats the motion.

My fingers dig into the delicious firmness of his butt and clutch him tighter. My ankles wrap around his lower legs, and I rock back into him with every thrust he makes.

I see stars.

This is more than a physical act. It's a claiming. Wyatt is

removing any other man from my memory, and I'm gladly allowing him to wipe the slate clean. From now on, there's only him. Only us. Only this beautiful way we move together.

I've never been so open or exposed before. His for the taking. It's as if he's made himself at home in my heart, and I never want him to leave.

His pelvis hits my clit, and the world concentrates down to a tiny pinpoint of sensation before it bursts apart. I cry his name, uninhibited, and he curses and shudders inside me.

"Felicity." His voice is a growl. "Damn, Felicity. I—" He breaks off as he comes, his teeth bared in a feral grimace. Then, he collapses onto his forearms, still holding most of his weight off me. He doesn't finish his sentence, and I'm curious to know what he was about to say but don't prod. Mostly because the intensity of what we just shared has left me in a state of euphoria.

"You can relax," I tell him. "Let me take your weight."

But he gets up and disposes of the condom instead. "Hold on a moment."

He leaves the room and returns a few seconds later with a damp washcloth. Tenderly, he cleans me, then takes care of himself. The heat of our encounter is fading, and I can't help but wish he'd never left the bed and created a sense of distance between us. As though reading my thoughts, he lies beside me and kisses my forehead.

His dark eyes fill with tenderness "That was... indescribable."

"It was amazing," I agree and wriggle closer, longing for him to take me in his arms. But he dithers. He looks unsure of what to do, and my heart squeezes. Does he think I don't want him here?

"Cuddle me?" I ask softly. "Stay with me?"

He nods, a shy smile crossing his face. It's heartbreaking in its sweetness. "As long as you want."

He pulls me close, and I rest my head on his chest, hearing the steady beat I've grown to adore. God, I hope he means it.

CHAPTER 12

WYATT

I PAUSE in the entry to the kitchen and enjoy the view. The cutest blonde I've ever had the pleasure to see naked stands in front of a skillet, nude except for my t-shirt, which falls down to her knees. Padding closer on quiet feet, I wrap my arms around her from behind and grin when she squeaks in surprise.

"Wyatt, you gave me a fright!"

I drop a kiss on her shoulder, where the neck of the t-shirt gapes open because she's so much smaller than me. "Whatcha cooking, beautiful?"

"Pancakes."

I peer at the batter that's slowly bubbling on the skillet. "Smells amazing."

"I was hoping to have them done before you woke up." She turns in my arms, and all the blood in my brain rushes south at the sight of her nipples pebbled against the fabric of my shirt. "Did you sleep well?"

"After two rounds of sex with my gorgeous girlfriend?" I ask, smiling at how sincere she is. "Yeah, I slept like the dead."

She shivers. "Ugh, don't even say that. Strikes too close to home for a horror writer."

I kiss her temple. "Let me make it up to you." I take her by the hips and lift her off the ground, placing her on the counter. She wraps her legs around my waist, my shirt riding up and showing me her pinkness. I press closer, taking in every detail. Her glossy lips and sultry eyes beg me to claim what I want. Dipping my head, I touch my lips to hers, drinking in the gasp that spills from them. But before I can take it any further, the acrid scent of burning fills my nostrils, followed closely by the shrieking of a smoke alarm. Felicity jumps like she's been shocked, and we both turn to the pan, where the pancake batter has shriveled and gone black around the edges.

"Crap." She pushes at my chest, and I back away. She leaps lightly to the floor and hurries to the skillet, taking it off the heat. I open a window and try to fan the smoke outside. As soon as the noise stops, my shoulders droop in relief. God, that thing is obnoxious.

Felicity giggles, and I glance at her, incredulous. She covers her mouth with a hand, her eyes dancing with amusement. "Guess we should have been paying attention, huh."

"I *was* paying attention," I grouch. "Just not to the food."

She turns red, nibbling on her lip. "Shall we try again?"

I sigh, tempted beyond belief by the prospect of picking up where we left off, but we need to eat at some point. "You do the pancakes, I'll make coffee."

She nods, then empties the burnt batter into the trash and starts again. I'm looking for milk when I hear a muttered, "uh oh."

"What is it?" I ask, checking to make sure she's all right and then scanning the room for trouble.

"Nadine is at your house."

Oh shit.

I follow her line of sight out the window toward my place just in time to see Mom knock on the back door. She must have already tried the front.

"*Wyatt*," Felicity hisses, her eyes wide. "What do we do?"

It seems the inevitable has arrived, so I just shrug. "We tell her. She's probably heard rumors by now anyway. Someone at the bar would have called to let her know about our performance. That's probably why she's here. To separate fact from fiction."

"But I'm practically naked," she protests.

I grin. "I know."

She sucks in a deep breath and is about to give me a piece of her mind when I beat her to the punch.

"Go get changed while I let her know I'm here." As she starts to turn away, I clear my throat. She glances over her shoulder, eyes like daggers. "Can I have my shirt?"

"Oh." She deflates, whips it over her head, and tosses it at me before dashing to the bedroom. I laugh, and it feels fucking amazing. That in itself tells me that coming clean is the right thing to do. Mom will be thrilled, and so am I. I sure as hell don't deserve Felicity, but I'm going to hold onto her and not let go.

I slip the t-shirt on, then open the window. "Hey, Mom."

She spins around, spots me in Felicity's window, and beams. "Well, it's about time."

Shaking my head, I ignore the bait. "Get over here. We're making pancakes."

While she crosses the lawn, I set the skillet back on the stove, turn the temperature down, and add batter to it. Felicity rushes into the kitchen moments before Mom arrives.

During the time she's been gone, she's pulled on a dress, tamed her hair into a ponytail, and donned a knitted purple cardigan that looks like it came from her grandmother's closet. Somehow, she makes it work. In two strides I'm at her side, and I lay a kiss on her that makes her blush like a schoolgirl.

"Aren't you two the cutest thing," Mom remarks from the doorway.

Felicity's already fiery cheeks turn an even deeper hue of red. "Hi, Nadine."

"Good morning, sweetheart." Her gaze flits between us, then a smile curves her mouth. "So, how long as this been going on?"

Releasing Felicity, I return to the pancakes. "By *this*, you mean?"

"The dating part." I can't see her face, but I picture it as I flip the pancake and take a moment to appreciate its golden brown underside. "I don't need to know anything about your sex life. I have enough nightmares already."

"About two weeks." I transfer the pancake to a plate and add more batter to the skillet.

"And when were you planning to tell me?" she demands. "I mean, it was obvious something was going on, but I had to hear about your romantic kiss in the square—and the duet you sang at Bender's—secondhand."

I wince, and pivot so I can see both women again. "Sorry about that."

"It's my fault," Felicity breaks in, and we both stare at her. Mom raises a brow. "I, uh, didn't want to tell people until we knew where things were heading."

I don't know why she's taking the fall for me. We never discussed whether to tell people or not. We've just been living in our own little bubble. But I appreciate her trying to take the heat, so I send her a smile of gratitude that lets her know exactly how I intend to thank her later.

Mom cocks a hip. "Have you figured it out yet?"

Felicity locks eyes with me, expression bordering on stricken. Our future isn't something we've talked about much, perhaps sensing that both of us are skittish and want to take things one day at a time.

"We're working on it," I reply. "But I care about her." My smile softens as I look at my girl. "So damn much."

"Excellent!" Mom pulls Felicity into a fierce hug and waggles her eyebrows at me behind her back. She separates from Felicity, a mischievous tilt to her smile that makes me nervous. "You should come to dinner on Sunday. We'd love to have you."

They would?

Something in my stomach tightens. I'm not sure what to think of the invitation. It's great that she and Julia are welcoming Felicity into the fold, but it's happening too fast. It took months for Mom to invite Dawn to dinner, and at that point we were in a committed, long-term relationship. Felicity and I aren't there yet, and it feels like the floor is shifting beneath my feet.

"I'd really like that," Felicity replies, practically bouncing on the spot. Of course she's happy about it. She likes to be included. To feel like she belongs. But I'm not a hundred percent sure she does yet. This niggling little voice in the back of my head tells me she's going to run and leave me piecing together the broken shards of my heart. "We'll be there, won't we, Wy?"

"Yeah." I swallow, trying to ignore the hard lump in my gut. "Guess so."

Felicity

Is it my imagination, or did Wyatt emotionally withdraw in the hours between yesterday morning, when Nadine showed up, and now, an hour before dinner with his family?

At first, I didn't think much of it. Of course he was going to be a bit quiet. His mother had caught us in the afterglow of sex, but I expected him to bounce back after she left, and he hasn't. It's making me nervous. He's uncommunicative enough under normal circumstances, but now he's all grunts and one-word answers. When I asked last night if he was okay, he said he was "fine."

Trust me, I know what 'fine' means.

But I'm trying not to dwell on it because I have to trust that he'll talk to me when he's ready. In the meantime, I have a dinner to prepare for. I scan the outfits laid out on my bed. Should I go for a pretty dress with heels to make a good impression? Or jeans and a blouse because the Dawson family doesn't stand on ceremony?

Ugh, I feel like this is a test I'm going to fail. I've always wanted to be part of a family, and this is my chance, but what if I mess it up?

Going to the wardrobe, I study its contents, then collect a floaty skirt and a cute tank top and add them to the growing pile of options. Holding up a pair of denim shorts, I consider how good my butt looks in them but deem them inappropriate for a family function. Frustrated, I grab my phone, snap a few photos, and send them to Wyatt.

Felicity: *What should I wear?*

The two minutes it takes him to reply feels like forever, and I begin to wonder if I should just drag him over here to have a look.

Wyatt: *Whatever you're comfortable in. My family won't care.*

"Could he be less helpful?" I mutter. Yeah, I'm probably over-thinking it, but a little direction would've been appreciated. I settle on the skirt and tank top because they're most *me*, but as I change into them, my mind veers off onto other concerns. Like food. Grabbing the phone again, I call him this time.

"Do I need to bring anything?" I ask as he picks up. "Like, dessert, maybe?"

"No." His tone indicates he's on edge. "Mom always makes enough to feed everyone twice over."

"Okay, but—"

"Sorry, Felicity, I'm midway through something." The call ends. Did he just hang up on me? I stare at the phone, my mouth hanging open. Perhaps he was midway through something that couldn't be paused for two minutes, but surely, he was more abrupt than necessary.

I head to the kitchen and pull two bottles of wine from the cupboard. I never have more than a couple because I rarely drink, but I think they're good quality, and it's only polite to take a gift when someone invites you for dinner. I read the label on each. Sauvignon Blanc or Pinot Noir? If I choose the wrong one, no one will drink it. Or worse, they'll feel obligated while secretly hating it. A bottle in each hand, I leave the kitchen and cross the lawn to Wyatt's place, where I let myself in the back entrance. He's sprawled on the sofa, watching a game of football and glances up as I enter. My fists clench around the necks of the bottles. Midway through something, huh?

"Sure, looks like you're busy."

He has the decency to wince. "I was fixing the bath-room plumbing a couple minutes ago."

"Sure." I'm not sure I believe him, but I know nothing about plumbing and how long it would take to fix something, so I don't push the matter. "Red or white?" I ask. "Which does Nadine prefer?"

"Red." He doesn't hesitate. "But you don't need to bring wine. I told you, everything is covered." He sounds a little snappish, and I back up a step. "All we need to do is turn up. Mom loves to play hostess."

"I just want to get this right," I tell him.

"I know." He sighs, then rubs a hand down his face. "You don't need to worry. She already loves you. So just take the wine home, get your bag, and come over here before you start wondering if you need to bring her flowers or some shit like that."

Ouch. I flinch.

His words aren't particularly mean-spirited, but there's an edge to them I don't like.

"I know I'm more nervous than most people would be," I say apologetically, because it's possible I'm annoying him with all my questions. "But this is new for me."

"You're fine."

There's that word again. *Fine.* God, I hate it.

"But for the record, we don't need to bring her flowers, a home-baked lasagna, or whatever else you're brewing in that pretty head of yours."

Double ouch. He may as well have patted me on said 'pretty head' and sent me on my way.

"Right. Well. Me and my pretty head will be next door, not bothering you." Biting my lip before I can say anything else, I spin on my heel and march out. Maybe he doesn't want wine, but I could certainly use a glass.

"Felicity!" He calls out, but I don't stop, and he doesn't follow.

I don't bother visiting again until I'm ready to go. He's in a weird mood, and I don't know how I'm supposed to deal with it when I don't know the cause, so I decide to act normal and hope to cheer him up.

When I return, he opens with, "Sorry for being short with you."

"It's fine." I shrug lightly, as if I don't hate the word 'fine' with every fiber of my being. "Let's get going."

Dinner is nice. As predicted, Nadine has enough food to serve most of the town. She and Julia are both in good spirits and chat while we eat. They make me feel welcome. Like I fit with them. Meanwhile, Wyatt remains quiet. He doesn't seem as broody as earlier, but he's not back to normal yet either. It's as though he's waiting for something bad to happen. When dinner is over, we play card games until he declares it time to go home.

We sit side by side in his truck, silence surrounding us, when he finally speaks. "Are we going to talk about it?"

"Talk about what?" I ask, surprised.

"Me snapping at you earlier. Ignoring it doesn't make it go away."

I study his profile in the dark cab, getting the impression he isn't trying to fix anything. He's looking to pick a fight. "You apologized, I accepted. What else is there to talk about?"

His fingers visibly tighten on the steering wheel. "The reason I was on edge in the first place."

Oh. So, he's going to broach it head on now. I didn't expect that because he seems the type of person to tiptoe around the edges of his feelings.

Reaching over, I rest a hand on his thigh to show my support. "Tell me."

He sighs and doesn't say anything for a long moment.

Meanwhile, a creeping sensation of dread crawls up my spine.

"Wyatt?"

"I'm scared," he admits so quietly I almost don't hear it.

My heart clenches. "Scared of what?"

He glances at me, and his eyes gleam in the darkness. "Of jumping into something too fast and everything falling apart." He wets his lips. "That's why I was a dick. I'm sorry. I just..." He takes a deep breath, his shoulders rising and falling. "Apparently, I have some hang-ups."

Forget clenching—my heart downright aches for him. But the wariness weighing on my shoulders doesn't go anywhere. Intentional or not, he just lumped me in with Dawn as someone who could hurt him. I'd never do that. I'm far too close to falling in love with him.

"I understand." I squeeze his thigh. "But you can trust me. I'm not going to let you and your big grumpy face scare me away."

A laugh tears through him, rusty and unexpected. "My big grumpy face?"

"It's a nice face," I assure him. "But a little pouty."

"*Pouty?*" He laughs incredulously. "Woman, I'll show you pouty."

I have no idea what he means by that, but he manages to imbue the word with sexual innuendo.

He pulls up outside his place and takes my hand. "Come inside and let me make it up to you."

"I'd like that." I smile tentatively, even though I have a niggling feeling that we haven't addressed everything we need to and it's going to come back to bite me in the butt.

CHAPTER 13

FELICITY

How ON EARTH did I think I could pull this off?

I stare at the to-do list I've written for myself and swallow hard. It's the day before the Fall Harvest and Crafts Festival, and I have dozens of things left to do in order to pull it off without a hitch. Talk about a tall order. I don't even know where to start. Some of these things are small and will only take ten minutes. Others are terribly daunting, and just thinking about them makes me want to curl up in a corner somewhere and refuse to engage with the world. Maybe if I ignore everything, it will magically happen without me.

"Why do you get yourself into these situations?" I mutter and rest my forehead on the kitchen counter. "You can't do this. What the heck do you know about planning a festival, anyway? But you're always putting your goddamn hand up."

The therapist I used to see told me that volunteering was my way of becoming 'part of the tribe.' Because apparently, I have a deep-rooted fear that I'm unlovable and will be rejected, which in caveman days would have meant death. These days, not so much, but try telling that to the lizard part of my brain.

Okay, okay. I stand up and pull myself together. I said I'd do this, which means I need a game plan, and for that I need someone who isn't caught in the same emotional whirlpool of overwhelm that I've found myself in. Grabbing my phone, I find Wyatt's number and call. It rings and rings, and for a few seconds I fear he won't answer, but then I hear the click of engagement.

"Hi, baby," he says, a muffled sound coming down the line as though he's holding the phone to his ear with his shoulder. "What's up?"

"I'm freaking out," I tell him.

Instantly, the muffled sound cuts off. "Felicity, take a deep breath," he says. "In through the nose, out through the mouth. You with me?"

I do as he says, and some of the tension eases from my chest. "With you."

"Okay, what's going on?"

"I just have so much to do." I sink to the floor and draw my knees to my chest. "There's ten million things to cross off my to-do list before tomorrow, and I have no idea how I'm going to handle it. I'm..." My throat threatens to close up with panic, and I inhale another slow breath, forcing it to relax. "I'm in over my head," I admit. "I was stupid when I offered to do this. I have no idea what I'm doing, and I'm going to fail because I didn't think ahead, just like always, and let everyone down. They're all going to hate me."

"Whoa, there." His voice is gentle. Soothing. Like a warm hug wrapping around me. "You've got this, gorgeous."

I sniff, mortified by the dampness of my eyes. "No, I don't."

"Yes," he assures me. "You do. You can do this, and

you're not alone. If you need help, Mom is available. She works for herself, so she can take a little time off to make sure you get things done, and she's not the only one. There are plenty who would be happy to pitch in. We're a community here, Felicity. That's how we do things."

I go all gooey inside. He hasn't fixed the problem, but hearing that he believes in me and that I'm not alone is a balm for my ego.

"Do you know what you need to do first?" he asks.

"No." I scan the list again, and my budding hope shrivels.

"Then you need to figure that out first. Hey," he adds, hearing my whimper of distress, "it's going to be all right. Go through your list and prioritize them into three groups. Stuff that's urgent, stuff you can do later, and stuff you might be able to let drop without it mattering too much. Think you can manage that?"

I nod, then remember he can't see me. "Yeah."

"Good." He's speaking to me the same way he might a skittish dog and it should annoy me, but frankly, I'm grateful. "I'll call Mom and mobilize the troops. She'll be over at your place soon."

"You'd do that?"

"Of course." There's another voice down the line—someone talking to him, perhaps. "I've got to go now, but call me if you need. I want to be there for you."

"Thank you." I could honestly cry with relief.

"No problem. You've got this, baby."

"Bye. I'll see you later."

"See you." As he hangs up, I hug my arms around my knees, my heart singing and tears streaming down my cheeks, and I don't even know why. But then, it hits me.

I'm in love with Wyatt.

He's everything I've ever wanted, wrapped into one brooding, sexy package. He's dependable, caring, and has roots. He treats me like I matter and makes me feel like I belong. I rest my forehead on my knees. I don't even have the energy to worry about the fact I've somehow tumbled into love with a man who hasn't indicated he feels the same way. I'm simply happy that I have him. Everything else can come later.

Wyatt

I HANG up and take my coffee and lunch from Ella, having been standing in line at Java by Jackie when Felicity called.

"Thanks." I smile and start for the door, but then a throat clears behind me. I freeze, and my back teeth lock together. I know that sound all too well.

"Tut tut," Dawn says, stepping alongside me. "That new girlfriend of yours is an emotional wreck."

"She's none of your business."

She smiles like a cat sizing up a sparrow. "I don't know what makes you believe you can hold onto her when you weren't even in touch with your emotions enough to hold onto me. I'm low maintenance compared to that hot mess."

"Whatever." Shaking myself out of the funk that paralyzed me, I continue toward the exit. The clacking of heels on the floor tells me that Dawn is following.

"Seriously, Wy," she says as the coffee shop door swings shut behind us. "You don't have it in you to give someone like her what she needs. You might as well just let her go now, before you get attached."

I'm already fucking attached.

I don't say the words, because Dawn is like a parasite, and once you give her a hint of what she wants, she'll suck you dry. I carry on walking.

"I'll be here when she gets tired of your emotional distance," she calls after me.

I sip my coffee even though it's scalding. The sharpness of it on my tongue keeps me in the present. I can't allow Dawn's comments to lead me down the rabbit hole of 'what ifs.' She's just being spiteful. Unfortunately, she has a point. If I didn't give someone like Dawn enough attention to stop her from seeking it elsewhere, how am I going to manage with Felicity? What if she needs more than I'm capable of giving?

Taking another mouthful of coffee, I don't even feel the burn. Felicity needs someone steady. Someone who can be her rock. She's never had that before. What if I mess up? Will she fall into her pattern of running and flit out of my life as easily as she flitted into it? I don't want to be left behind, nursing a broken heart. What Dawn did messed me up, but if Felicity ran away, I'm not sure I'd recover.

CHAPTER 14

FELICITY

THE SCENT OF APPLE PIE, fried food, and cotton candy fills the air. The festival has only been running for ten minutes, but people are already beginning to arrive. The vendors are situated in a grid pattern in the center of the town square. Food booths are clustered in one area, crafts in another, games along an outer edge, and the booths for the apple pie and largest pumpkin contests occupy pride of place in the middle of everything. Beside them, a guy sits on a stand playing guitar and crooning into a microphone. He's one of three local acts who have been booked to perform over the course of the day.

Wyatt wraps an arm around my waist. "It's all going to work out because of you."

"Because of your mom," I correct him, but he shakes his head.

"No, this is all on you. Mom and her friends only did what you told them to."

I flush, unused to compliments—especially about my accomplishments—and unsure how to handle it.

"Felicity," someone calls, and I scan the faces until I spot one of the volunteers I roped into helping me judge and police the pumpkin contest. I join her, Wyatt at my side. She's standing with a ruddy-cheeked gentleman who has the rangy build of a man who works outdoors. "This is Tyrone Autry. He's filed a complaint against Margaret Adams."

"You're the organizer?" Tyrone's cheeks grow even redder as he looks me up and down. By my side, Wyatt stiffens, but I run a hand up his arm to soothe him.

"I am." I offer a brisk handshake. "What seems to be the problem, Mr. Autry?"

"I'm not tryin' to make trouble." By now, his face is an unusual shade of scarlet. "But Margaret stole my pumpkin while I wasn't looking and replaced it with an inferior one." He folds his arms over his wiry chest. "And I can prove it."

I fight the urge to giggle, pleased that Wyatt warned me how competitive these pumpkin-growers could be. The day is sure to be nothing if not interesting. "Please, by all means, show me your evidence."

He leads me away, and fifteen minutes later, the situation is resolved. The festival continues in much the same fashion. Minor crises arise, and I deal with them. Meanwhile, everyone enjoys themselves. The music is upbeat, the food—or what little I get to taste of it—is delicious, and the locals all seem to be in the mood for celebration. Through everything, Wyatt stays by my side. I try to wave him off a few times, not wanting to dominate his day, but he just tags along, and by evening, I feel like I could conquer the world. There isn't a thing that could crop up that I can't deal with.

A hand snags mine, a callused palm rubbing against my own, setting my hormones alight. I smile over my shoulder at Wyatt as he tugs me close. His lips meet mine, and my smile lasts throughout our kiss. I simply can't shut it off.

"You're amazing," he murmurs, smoothing my hair back from my face. He cradles my chin as though no one else is around, even though half the township could see us if they cared to look. "You've been brilliant today. You should be proud of yourself."

Warmth steals into my heart and radiates out until it consumes my entire body. I throw my arms around him and hug him tight. "Thank you. I couldn't have done it without you." Drawing back, I notice the upward hitch of his mouth. The one I adore with every fiber of my being. His barely-there smile is all for me. "I love you."

His expression shutters. His hands drop away, and he stuffs them into his pockets. I can't read what's going on inside his head, but I feel his withdrawal to the core of my being.

"You're amazing," he repeats, and then reaches for my hand to kiss the back of it. The warmth in my chest dies a swift death, and my cheeks flood with heat. I lower my eyes, embarrassed. I just confessed my love, and he can't do the same.

Well, this is awkward.

"Thanks." I look around, praying for someone to need my assistance. One of the women running a card-making stall sees me and waves. I act like she's gestured me over, and nod toward her. "I'd better..." I hurry away, and he follows behind, the same way he's been doing all day. But this time, I wish he'd leave me alone. Just for a while.

Too soon, I get my wish. His friends turn up, and after checking with me, Wyatt leaves to sample the array of apple pies. It takes only five minutes for Dawn to hunt me down, alone and unprotected. The smug smirk she's wearing gives me the impression she's been circling like a hyena, waiting for the opportunity to strike.

"Poor Felicity," she says, pouting nastily. "Wyatt isn't an easy guy to know, and it seems like you're starting to figure that out."

"Wyatt and I are fine," I tell her, then wince at hearing the word 'fine' come out of my mouth. "Great, actually. But thanks for your concern."

She tosses her hair over her shoulder and cocks a hip. "No, you're not, and it's truly sad that you think you can pretend." Any attempt to appear friendly is long gone. I'm seeing her without her mask, and it's ugly. "You're not up to the challenge." She scoffs and shakes her head. "You walk around here like you're so much better than everyone else, but you're just a silly little girl who doesn't know how to hold onto a man like Wyatt."

"You're wrong." I stand my ground, even though I'm quivering in my ballet flats. "I love him, and I'm not going anywhere. I'm going to make him much happier than you and your unfaithful heart ever could."

Her jaw drops. It's oddly satisfying. I turn and stride away before she can think of a retort, because I don't have the energy to go another round. But even though I'm proud of fighting back, her words eat at me. After all, he did ignore my declaration of love. Maybe I'm not what he really wants.

No, Felicity. Don't listen to her. He cares about you; he just needs time.

I can give him time. Right?

Wyatt

SHE LOVES ME. Holy hell. I'm not sure what I'm supposed to do with that.

Hours later, when the festival has wound down, I'm still buzzing from her confession. I'm torn between being thankful for having the love of a woman like Felicity, feeling guilty for not being able to reply in kind, and scared that despite everything, she might not be around for the long haul.

Mostly, the guilt wins out. She told me she loved me, and I couldn't say it back. She might have played it cool, but I could see it hurt her, so I need to do what I can to show how I feel with my actions. Hopefully, that will be enough.

Smiling, I cross the courtyard to her side, cup her face between my hands, and kiss her. She softens into my embrace, and the corners of her lips lift as she smiles against my mouth.

"Hey." I draw back and tuck her hair behind her ear. After being on the go all day, it's a cloud of white fluff around her shoulders.

"Hi, you." Her expression is tentative.

"You did good," I tell her. "Everyone had a wonderful day."

She rests her cheek on my chest and wraps her arms around me. "Thanks. I'm exhausted."

Chuckling, I hold her close. "So, you don't want to go out for dinner?"

Her chin tilts up. "Go out where?"

"How about the Farm Barn? It's an organic restaurant on the outskirts of town. They grow everything they cook onsite. Interested?"

"Oh, my gosh!" Her eyes light up. "Yes. That sounds delicious. Just give me half an hour to shower and change my clothes."

"Done. Come on." Taking her hand, I lead her to my truck. We drive home, and I head over to my place while she goes to hers. While the Farm Barn isn't the kind of place where you dress fancy, I want to look my best for her. She deserves it. So, I put on dark jeans, a button-down shirt, and my shiniest black shoes. I even wash my face and spray on a little cologne. Then, I lock up and stroll across the darkening yard and sit on her doorstep in the cool dusk air. When she joins me, she smells of flowers and shampoo, and she's dressed in a pale purple skirt with a black jersey and glossy lips. I climb to my feet and drop a kiss on her cheek.

"You're beautiful, sweetheart." I don't mention that she'd look even more beautiful in one of my shirts and nothing else. Hopefully, the night will end that way.

"You're very sharp, too." She reaches around me and pinches my butt. "What's the occasion?"

"We're celebrating you." I guide her to the truck, open the door, and help her in. "Good food, great booze, and the best company. What more could you want?"

Something flickers behind her eyes. Something a little dark, as though she's thought of something she'd rather not, and I can't help but hope she doesn't see this for what it is: me trying to smooth over what could be perceived as an earlier rejection. I circle the truck and slide in, starting the engine. Once we're on the road, I offer her my hand and keep a hold of hers while we cruise out of town, past the trees by the lake, and all the way to the drive that veers off toward the Farm Barn.

"It looks charming," she says as we park outside. "Do you come here often?"

I get out and hurry around to open her door. "Uh, no. It's not really my scene, but I think you'll like it."

"Aww." She goes onto her toes and kisses me softly. "Thank you."

I don't feel worthy of her, so I don't reply, just hunch my shoulders and usher her inside, where a woman in a blazer greets us and shows us to our seats. I called and booked a table earlier because this isn't the kind of place where you can walk in and be assured of a spot.

"Can I get you something to drink?" the woman asks, smiling at Felicity before turning to me with a raised brow. I order a hot chocolate, and Felicity requests a decaf latte. When the woman leaves, my girl opens a menu and scans the options. I watch her, noting the way her forehead crinkles as she thinks. God, she's adorable. Small, delicate nose. Lips that are constantly raised at the edges, ready to break into an expression of joy. She's the kind of woman I'd be lucky to have in my life, but as much as I want to believe her declaration, and be secure in our budding relationship, doubt chips away at my faith.

"What do you recommend?" she asks.

"Nope." I mime zipping my lips. "I'm not influencing your decision. If you choose the wrong thing, that's on you."

She laughs but rolls her eyes. "Okay, fine. I think I want... the sweetcorn risotto."

"Good choice." I nod approvingly. "And for dessert?"

She shakes her head. "I'm not committing to dessert until I know for sure I'll have room."

"Oh, you'll make room. Trust me."

Her lips curve wider. "Are you going to insist?"

I nod seriously. "I'm afraid I'll have to."

"Well, okay then." She checks the menu again. "I'll have nested meringue with peach sorbet."

"Chocolate heaven for me. All the way." Leaning closer,

I murmur, "The only thing that could make it better is licking the chocolate sauce off your body."

Her eyes widen, pupils eclipsing the hazel irises, and she licks her lips. "You know, I saw a stand by the counter where you can buy the chocolate sauce for your own use. We're definitely taking some home."

I gulp. My dick stirs, and I glance at the ceiling, willing it to calm down. Why am I not jumping into the deep end with both feet when it comes to this girl? She's one of a kind.

"You're going to enjoy every second of it," I promise.

A waitress comes to take our orders, and after she leaves, I make small talk, asking about the book Felicity is writing, which she doesn't like to discuss—something about damaging the creative process. We chat about how she started writing and when she first knew she could make a career of it—early on, because she lives frugally and managed to get through school without much debt.

When dinner arrives, she enjoys it as much as I hoped she would, oohing and aahing over the flavors, her face lighting up with each mouthful. The dessert is even better. For the first time I can recall, I'm less interested in my chocolate heaven than I am in the company. She excuses herself to the restroom when she finishes, and I head up to the counter to take care of the bill. Felicity narrows her eyes when she returns and realizes I've paid for us both, but she lets me escort her outside without argument. We pause by the truck, reluctant to get in because it means we're nearing the end of the night.

"I've enjoyed this," she says, smiling up at me as though I personally harvested the sweetcorn for her risotto. "Thanks for bringing me here. We'll have to come back sometime."

Will she be around to come back with me?

Shutting down the unwanted question, I draw her to my chest. "Anytime you want, sweetheart." Then, I kiss her. Deep, slow, and drugging. She tastes of peaches and sugar, and I hold onto her with a kind of desperation that should be a big red flag, but I can't bring myself to care.

CHAPTER 15

WYATT

"Coffee?" I ask Felicity, who is curled on my sofa, her feet tucked beneath her and a blanket over her lap.

"No, thanks," she says. "But I'll have a chamomile tea."

I nod. Thanks to her, I do actually have that in my cupboard. Food has been slowly migrating from her pantry to mine, and I can't lie—I like it. Even if things have erred on the side of awkward for the past few days because of the whole L-word situation, I enjoy having her around. She makes me feel light inside, as if a weight has been lifted. She makes me smile and want to be optimistic about the future, but I'm worried that if I relax and let go, the rug will be ripped out from under me.

I boil the kettle and make a mug of chamomile tea for Felicity and an instant coffee for myself, then carry them to the living room.

"Make some room," I say, slipping under the blanket beside her.

She takes her tea and sets it aside, then rests her head on my shoulder. "This is really nice."

"It is," I agree.

"It's so cozy." Her breast is soft against the side of my arm, and I wrap an arm around her, my palm curving around the dip of her waist. "All that's missing is the roaring fire."

"Yeah, I don't have one of those." Although with the way the weather is today, I wouldn't mind joining her in front of one.

A knock sounds on the front door. I meet Felicity's eyes.

"Are we expecting anyone?" she asks.

"Not that I know of." I kiss the tip of her nose, loving her use of the word 'we.' "Are you gonna make me get it?"

Her lips curve mischievously. "It's your house."

"Fine." I heave an exaggerated sigh and disentangle myself from her and the blanket. I open the front door to find Julia standing on the porch, cheeks red from the cold wind and a beanie pulled low over her ears. "Hey, Jules. Come in."

"Thanks." She shuffles past me and down the hall. "Oh, hey." She smiles at Felicity, who's still on the sofa. "Sorry to barge in like this."

"You're always welcome here," I tell her, and Felicity nods.

"Great." She settles onto the spot beside my girl, where I'd previously been. I sit on a chair across the room. "It's actually you I was looking for," she continues to Felicity. "I finished reading Chased by Darkness. Horror isn't my usual genre, although I read a little now and then. I'm more of a sci-fi geek. Still, I had to come over and say, *whoa*. Talk about intense. That was one of the most twisted books I've ever read. Your mind is a seriously dark place."

Uh oh. Julia doesn't realize it, but she just stepped in a pile of crap.

Felicity's lips press together, and I can visibly see her

shut down. Almost subconsciously, she shuffles away from Julia, and her usually easy-to-read expression becomes carefully blank. "It's really not," she mutters. "I just have a good imagination."

Julia beams, failing to read the non-verbal cues. What Felicity doesn't realize is that to Julia, 'twisted' is a compliment. She loves things that are out of the ordinary. "Whatever you want to call it, I've never read anything so freaking screwy."

Felicity grabs her phone and scans the screen as though someone has just messaged. They haven't, because her ringtone is loud enough to be heard from another room, but I don't call her on it. Perhaps she needs a little time to gather herself and see that Julia means well—it's her own personal history and bias determining how she receives the words. But then, she pushes the blanket off and stands.

"I've got to go make a phone call. I might be a while." She glances at Julia. "It was nice to see you." Her legs carry her out of the room so fast she must be nearly running.

"What was that about?" Julia asks as the door slams shut to mark her exit.

"Damn." I get to my feet. "She left her last place because they ostracized her after reading her books. I know you meant what you said as a compliment, but she doesn't, and it's a bit of a sore point."

"Oh, no!" Her face falls, and she looks aghast. "I didn't know it would upset her. Honestly, I loved it. I'm going to go over there right now and—"

"No," I interrupt, before she has the chance to launch an offensive and freak Felicity out even more. "You wait here. I'll talk to her."

"She should hear it from me."

"And she can. After." I grab my jacket from over the back of a nearby chair and shrug it on. "Be back soon."

As I follow Felicity out into the cold, I can't help wondering if it's always going to be like this. Her running, and me chasing. I don't want to spend my life putting out fires.

Instead of going to the front door, which is no doubt locked, I let myself in the back and find her in the bedroom. Her arms are around herself, and she's shivering. Whether from cold or something else, I don't know.

"I'm sorry," she says as I sit on the edge of the bed. "I just couldn't listen for any longer."

"You weren't really listening at all," I tell her gently. "If you'd paid attention rather than jumping to conclusions, you could have saved yourself the shitty emotions you're going through now."

Her eyes flash—a spark of anger amid the misery. Good, she needs to feel something other than sorry for herself. "Excuse me, but it was *your* sister who said I have a dark and twisted mind."

"She meant it as a positive thing," I explain. "Jules loves all things dark and twisted."

"She does?" Her voice is soft. Uncertain.

"Yeah, baby." Reaching over, I lay a hand on her thigh to calm her. "She isn't going to reject you because of what you write. Quite the contrary. She'll probably become your biggest advocate and get all her friends reading it."

She blinks, and her lashes glimmer with unshed tears. "How can you be sure of that?" Her lips wobble, and she forces them into a firm line to still the tremor. "Maybe there really is something wrong with me."

I'm torn between sympathy and frustration. "There's not. You're the sweetest, kindest person I know."

"But am I?" she asks, burying herself deeper in a cocoon of self-pity. "Or is that just how it seems on the outside?"

I sigh. "There's not much I can do for you if you're not willing to believe in yourself."

She sits up straighter, forehead creasing in surprise.

"You have to learn not to run every time something gets under your skin," I continue, knowing that she needs to hear this even though she'd clearly prefer not to. "Problems and emotions aren't things you can run from forever."

"That's not what I'm doing," she argues, scrambling off the bed on the far side and facing me with her hands clenched at her sides.

"Yeah, it is. And I get it. You haven't had many people you can trust, and when you've fallen, the landing has been hard. But it won't be like that here. And I'm afraid that if you don't realize that, I'm going to be left heartbroken when we hit a bump in the relationship. Especially if you decide it's easier to run away and start over than put in the effort to figure it out."

Felicity

IF WYATT HAD SLAPPED me in the face, it couldn't have hurt more.

He thinks I'm going to break his heart? All because I have a painful past and don't like conflict? I can't believe what I'm hearing. I *know* I tend to move on if things don't work out—I've lived in over a dozen places, after all—but I've had good reason to leave each and every one of them, and I've never broken anyone's heart when I left. Half the time, the situation was out of my hands, and the other times... Well, who would stay where they aren't wanted? Going somewhere new makes me smart and adaptable, not a coward.

"I'm not the one here who's scared of their emotions." My voice is so fraught with tension that I hardly recognize it. "You're right that I don't trust easily, but you wouldn't either if you'd been uprooted over and over again. It's easier not to get attached. But I'm trying. I'm putting myself out there for you. I want this to work. It seems like you're using a minor thing to push me away."

"Push you away?" He scoffs. "All I want is to keep you here. You're the one who continues to run."

"No," I say, warming to the topic. "Think about it. I told you that I love you, and you couldn't even acknowledge it because you're afraid of having something real with me and getting hurt again if it doesn't work out. I'm not like Dawn. I won't turn my back on you the way she did. I might need a little space to deal with things sometimes, but I want to stay with you through thick and thin."

He stands, and crosses his arms over his broad chest, his expression bordering on petulant. "I'm not so sure you will stay."

I round the bed, coming to a stop in front of him. While I don't like conflict—and this feels an awful lot like conflict—we need to get everything out in the open. If doubts have been simmering beneath the surface for him, it's better for both of us if we air them.

"Why?"

He shifts from one foot to the other, clearly uncomfortable. "Because you're trying so hard to carve out a place for yourself here and make yourself fit, but one day you might decide it's not worth the effort or that you don't fit the way you wanted to. What's to stop you from driving away and starting over?"

I fall back a step and feel the blood drain from my face. Is he saying this is a square-peg-round-hole scenario? Because I thought I'd been fitting into Oak Bend perfectly, but it doesn't sound like he agrees. "I'm not trying to squeeze myself into a place that doesn't fit, and I won't force myself on anyone who doesn't want me." Shoving past him, I race for the exit, unwilling to let him see me cry, but he grabs my shoulder as I pass. I shake him off and stumble into the hall.

"Felicity!" he calls behind me. "I didn't mean it that way."

I don't wait to hear how he did mean it, because I have no desire to listen to him detail all the ways I've gone about things wrong. I round the corner at the end of the hall into the living area and pass through it in a few steps. The sound of his footfalls follow as I hurry toward the back door.

"You're doing it again!" he yells. "Running away from a hard conversation."

Ignoring him, I cross the lawn to my car and lock myself in before driving to the coffee shop. Am I hiding? Yeah, maybe. But screw him; he's hiding, too.

CHAPTER 16

WYATT

UNSURE WHETHER I just won or lost an argument, I return to my place. The wind kicks up, and I shiver, guilt seeping through me. Felicity wasn't wearing much. Hopefully wherever she's going, it'll be warm. Our words replay in my mind. Shit, I was a dick to her with all those accusations. But I can't bring myself to regret it—even if I don't like the outcome—because I'm right to be concerned by her response to stressful situations. It's not out of the realm of possibility to think she might run away after a disagreement and decide it's easier not to come back. Like now. For most people, this would be a tiff. Nothing to end a relationship over. But when it comes to her, I'm not sure where we stand. In her mind, is it over? Or is this just a bump in the road?

I hate that I even have to wonder.

"How is she?" Julia asks as I let out a huff and collapse on the couch. I just shake my head. "Did you tell her I didn't mean to upset her?"

I nod.

Her eyes narrow. "What else did you say? There's something you're not telling me."

My mouth is so dry I'm not sure I could speak if I wanted to. I stare at my hands, which are callused from work, and curl my fingers tightly into my palm.

"Wyatt?" she prompts.

"I might have said she couldn't keep running from things she didn't like and implied that I didn't trust her not to do that to me."

"Oh, God." She rubs her temples and groans. "*Men*. How are you all so dense at times?"

"It's a real concern."

She glares at me, and I glare right back.

"She's sensitive," she says. "It takes time to build confidence in a new relationship."

"According to her, I'm the one who's sensitive." I scoff. "Yeah, right."

Julia looks pained. "Maybe you kinda are."

"You can't be serious."

She shrugs apologetically. "You don't wear your heart on your sleeve, but you experience things deeply. Why don't you tell me exactly what she said?"

I bury my face in my hands. I don't want to have this conversation. Why do women insist on dissecting things? I've let Felicity know where I stand. Can't we just quit talking about it and see what happens next?

"Hey." Her weight settles onto the seat beside me. "I'm here to listen. You know if I have to choose sides, I'm on yours. That's what being family means."

"Ugh, fine. She said I'm trying to push her away."

"And are you?" The question is gentle, but firm.

"Of course not," I mutter. "She was being ridiculous. She's the one who keeps running."

"Mmhmm." She doesn't sound like she entirely agrees. "Is that before or after you give her a shove?"

I toss my head back and stare at the ceiling, wishing that someone would just be straight with me for once instead of talking in fucking metaphors. "I might have made a couple of unnecessary comments, but for the most part, it all needed to be said."

"Mmhmm," she murmurs again. Damn, she has this shrink thing down. "But did it need to be said *now*, or could it have waited until you were both in a calmer frame of mind?"

I don't answer, because she might have a point. "Can't you just go away and leave me to wallow in peace?"

To my surprise, she stands. "Just take notice of what you're doing, Wyatt. I'm trying to help, and you're pushing me away." She lays a hand on my shoulder. "I love you, and I'm undoubtedly on your side, but make sure you glance in a mirror from time to time, okay? You might be shocked by what you see looking back at you."

"Sure, whatever." I don't have the mental bandwidth to unravel her prettily worded advice, but I'll agree to anything if it means I can have a few moments free of psychoanalysis.

"Bye." She kisses the top of my head. "Love you. Call me if you need."

"Bye." I raise a hand to wave as she leaves, then stretch out on the couch and wonder if there are many people at Benders.

Not long after, I have my answer. Very few. I'm grateful for the quiet as I sit in the corner furthest away from the bar with a beer and gaze into its amber depths. What was I thinking to fall for someone as flighty as Felicity? I should have seen disaster coming from day one. It's not as if the clues weren't there.

As I drink, I ponder Julia's words. She seems to think I'm partially responsible for the situation I find myself in, and much as I'd rather not, I have to agree. If I'd just listened to my gut and stayed away from Felicity to begin with, we wouldn't have found ourselves in this push-and-pull relationship.

Here's another reluctant truth: I *have* been pushing her away. Perhaps it's subconscious, but that doesn't make it any less real. And yeah, I know she's not Dawn. She's *worse*. Because Dawn and I were together for much longer, but I never felt half as torn up over her as I do now. Her actions were a blow to my ego, and her accusation that it was all my fault made me wary of beginning anything new, but the actual loss of Dawn didn't break my heart the way losing Felicity might.

Have I already lost her? I'm afraid to wonder. Yet another good reason to be here, where I can't see her if she decides she's had enough of Oak Bend and packs her bags to leave. I don't think I could watch that without doing something worse than hurling a few hurtful statements.

Like beg her to stay.

Better for us both if I have another drink and don't move from this bar stool.

Felicity

AFTER DEMOLISHING a piece of pie from the diner because the coffee shop is closed at this time of night, I head home, park on the road and scan for signs of Wyatt before dashing to the house. It's freezing inside because I'd intended to be over at Wyatt's all night, so I hadn't bothered to warm it up. There's a knock on the front door, and I freeze, heart pounding, but then remember I locked it. Thank God. I can't deal with anyone right now.

"Felicity," a voice calls. "It's Julia. Open up!"

I ignore her, pretending I'm not home even though I know she can see my car out front. She probably waited until I arrived to come over, but that doesn't mean I have to let her in. She's the one who started all of this, even if it was unintentional. I cringe, recalling her words. Does she actually believe my mind is dark and twisted? Because I really don't see how that can be said in a good way.

"I'm sorry!" she yells. "I didn't mean to upset you. Can we talk?"

I still don't answer because I can't bear to face her. Closing my eyes, I rest my forehead on the hallway wall. A memory leaps into my mind with perfect clarity. Meredith, the woman who'd treated me like a long-lost daughter, with an expression of horror as she held a copy of my latest release and demanded to know what was wrong with me. Tears threaten, and I squeeze my eyes more tightly to hold them in. I don't want to revisit that moment, which is why I can't open the door. There's only so much rejection a woman can take.

I move on autopilot and somehow find myself in my bedroom, my suitcase on the bed and the closet open. I toss things into it. The dress I was wearing when Wyatt and I first slept together. The pretty lingerie I bought this week and was so excited to show him. I pile underwear on top, then skirts, jerseys, and everything I can get my hands on until it's overflowing. I cram it shut, then fill the other suitcase with the belongings that are spread around the house. Toiletries. A few books. Some snacks from the kitchen. The non-perishables can stay here. It doesn't take long because

I've done this routine so many times that it barely warrants any thought.

Checking to make sure Julia is gone, I inch open the door and drag my suitcases through it. Locking up takes a few seconds, and then I'm sitting in the driver's seat of my car, the engine going, staring at the dark street ahead.

What am I doing?

We had an argument—that's all. And yet, here I am with my suitcases packed, ready to run. My fingers grip the steering wheel. The only thing I accomplish if I hit the county road out of town is reinforcing Wyatt's opinion of who I am. And then what? What happens when I get close to someone in the next town and they say something I take the wrong way? Will I move on again in a never-ending cycle of relocation? I'm like one of those sharks that can't stop swimming or they'll die. Will I forever be chasing something that doesn't exist, losing all of the good things that come along because I don't have the courage to stand my ground and face my fears?

I don't want to leave Oak Bend. From the quirky locals to the peaceful writing spots, the karaoke nights, and the greasy burgers at Mickey's Diner, I love this place. And I shouldn't have to go. I've been up front with people about who I am and what I do from the beginning. I haven't hidden anything, and I have nothing to be ashamed of. I drop my hands from the steering wheel to my lap and flex my fingers to ease their rigidity. Then, I dig in my purse for my phone and check the time. It's after 9pm. Where did I think I was going to go this late anyway?

A message from Julia pops up on the screen. My breath catches, and my stomach turns over.

Julia: *I loved your book. I'm so sorry I wasn't clear about that. It was absolutely genius. When I said dark and twisted,*

I meant that in the best possible way. I just want to climb inside your brain and have a look around to see where you get such freaking awesome ideas.

P.S. You hit the nail on the head with Wyatt. He's terrified of being hurt again. I'm sorry if he was a dick to you.

P.P.S. Be careful with him.

There's so much within one message that I don't know how to react. Apparently, Wyatt was telling the truth. 'Dark and twisted' is a compliment from Julia. I have no idea how, but go figure. I roll my neck from side to side, some of the kinks easing out. At least that's one less thing to worry about. If I'd only stopped and listened to her, I could have avoided the ugliness that followed. Regret washes over me. I may have been correct about Wyatt's fears when I lashed out at him, but he was spot-on with his accusations, too. I started running without taking the time to realize I didn't need to. Taking a breath, I type a message back.

Felicity: *Thanks for texting. I'm sorry I overreacted. It's a sore point for me. As for Wyatt, I don't know if he wants much more to do with me. I screwed up.*

I glance at the house beside mine. It's empty, and the lights are off. He must have gone somewhere. The way he sounded as he called after me echoes in my mind, clear as day. He was annoyed but resigned too. As if he'd already given up on us.

But that doesn't mean *I* have to give up on us.

Julia: *Trust me, he wants you, but you'll need to be patient with him.*

Sighing, I grab the lever that controls the incline of the seat and shift it back until I'm almost horizontal. Through the windows, stars sparkle amid the darkness.

I can be patient with Wyatt. I can prove to him that I'm

here for the long haul and that I'm serious about changing my pattern of running.

Felicity. *Thanks for the advice. XX*

Julia: *So you're not leaving?*

Felicity: *No, I'm here to stay.*

Julia: *That's what I like to hear. My pig-headed brother needs you. See you soon.*

I return the phone to my purse and stare at the stars for a while longer. Then, I carry my suitcases inside, unpack my belongings, and sit at my laptop to write an excessively violent scene. It's cathartic. While a big part of me wants to call Wyatt and talk things through, I don't. I can talk until I'm blue in the face, but it won't prove anything to him. The best way to show him I'm not running is to live my life as normal.

He'll come around, won't he?

CHAPTER 17

WYATT

When one of the guys from Benders drops me home, a little worse for wear, the light is still on next door. I stand on the porch in the dark and stare at the glow coming through the window. Does it mean she's not leaving? That I haven't driven her away? Or is it merely that she's waiting until morning to go, which would be the more sensible thing to do?

I'm just tipsy enough to think I should talk to her, and I've made it all the way to her door and raised a fist to knock before I realize what a monumentally stupid idea that is. If sober me couldn't fix the situation, there's no way that drunk me can, and I don't think she'd appreciate me pouring out my heart in my current state. Besides, she'll probably be gone soon, anyway.

But by the time morning rolls around and I drag my slightly hungover ass out to my truck, her car is still parked beside the sidewalk. I glance at the house to make sure she's not looking, then peer in the vehicle windows. No suitcases. Perhaps, like me, she needs time to recover from last night before leaving Oak Bend in her rearview mirror.

In the evening, she's still there. She doesn't visit, though, and I'm too unsure of myself to go to her. What would I even say? I don't know whether to apologize or not. Yeah, I behaved badly, but I believe in my heart that I spoke the truth. Uncertain of myself, I keep my distance.

The next day, she's still there. And the day after that.

By this point, I have no idea what to do. I accused her of running, then basically pushed her to do just that, yet she hasn't left. Does she want to work things out? If that were the case, wouldn't she have said something? Instead, there's been radio silence between us. No texts. No calls. No late-night dessert visits or waving through the windows. The one time I spotted her, she glanced away before I had time to react, apparently not interested in engaging.

I miss her.

I didn't realize how much I would until I had to spend a night in my bed without her. My queen-size bed, that's big enough for two people. I miss the scent of her hair, the sound of her laugh, and her way of making me smile. Life without her feels so much heavier. Perhaps that's an odd choice of word, but it's the most apt one I can think of. Everything requires more effort than before. My feet are weighted with lead for each step I take, and an atmosphere of loneliness seems to press in on me.

How am I supposed to undo the damage we did to each other? It's too late to take back the things I said, and she's sensitive, like one of those flowers with delicate petals that fall off if you touch them the wrong way. I'm worried that I metaphorically manhandled her with my rough fingers and bruised her delicate petals. Crushed them in my fist.

At least I have lunch with Mom and Julia today to distract me. After making a concerted effort not to gaze longingly at the house next door, I drive over to their place.

Mom is cooking, thank God. Delicious aromas float around me as I line my shoes up at the door and step inside.

"You look terrible," Julia remarks from her vantage point at the dining table.

"Thanks, Jules. I'm operating on four hours of sleep."

"Is it because you messed things up with Felicity and have to live with the knowledge that you're an idiot?"

"Hey, now," Mom chides from the kitchen. "Play nice, children."

"Well, he is," she mutters, facing me. "I love you and all, but you thought she'd leave and she proved you wrong by staying. Now you still haven't mended the fences."

"She didn't run *this* time," I agree. "But what about next? Maybe it's better we aired our differences before either of us got really attached."

She raises a brow. "Are you telling me you aren't already attached?"

I ignore her, knowing she wants to bait me into reacting.

"Food is ready!" Mom calls, and we both make our way to the kitchen counter, where three plates are waiting to go.

"Oh, darling." Mom frowns at me. "You look poorly. I don't know the whole story, but could there be some truth to what Jules is saying?"

"It doesn't matter." I can hear the self-pity in my voice and hate it. When did I become whiny? "I hurt Felicity, and I regret that. I... I miss her, but she's not reliable, and after what happened with Dawn, I need someone steady."

"Of course you do," Mom agrees. "But perhaps you need to trust that steadiness will come if you're patient. It sounds like you're both recovering from difficult rejections, and healing isn't instantaneous, however much we might want it to be."

We sit around the table, and I consider her words while

she says grace. Perhaps she's right, and I expected too much of Felicity too soon. Maybe I need to give her time. I stay quiet while we eat homemade chicken pasties and fried vegetables, mulling things over.

"Do you think Felicity would betray you the way Dawn did?" Mom asks cautiously.

"Well, no," I admit. "Not like that." The fact that she'd even ask makes me want to go out to bat for Felicity, and I pause when I realize that's exactly what Mom intended. I'm torn between laughing and swearing because her mind games are that good. Instead, I give myself a moment to collect my thoughts. "But if she lets me fall in love with her and then abandons me when things get hard, she may as well have cheated because it'll hurt the same."

"Honey." Mom's tone is gentle. "I think it's too late to protect yourself by trying to push her away. You already love her."

I start to deny it but can't make myself say the words. Goddamn, she might be right. If love means feeling sick at the thought of being without the other person, then I've caught the bug. The problem is, I don't know what to do about it.

"Have you ever considered that, if she did decide to leave, you could go with her?" The question comes from Julia and totally blindsides me.

No, I haven't.

But why not? I could move. As a brick mason, I can work anywhere. That's the benefit of having a trade. Why has it not crossed my mind until now? Could it be that I didn't want to consider the possibility because it would put responsibility for the success of our relationship on my shoulders when I'd rather stick my head in the sand and blame Felicity if it all goes to shit?

Hell. I have this nasty feeling that I'm equal parts to blame for our argument the other day, which means I need to do something about it, unless I want our stalemate to continue.

"I'll think about it," I tell Julia.

Hours later, when I'm preparing dinner, I glance out the window and see Felicity on her hands and knees in the garden. My first instinct is to go to her. Once again, she's pulling things out with abandon, failing to differentiate flowers from weeds. I laugh. Much as I know she'd love to think of herself as a domestic goddess, she's completely useless when it comes to gardening. Honestly, it's endearing. She looks so serious as she grips a plant I know Mom intentionally cultivated, studies it from different angles, then shakes her head and yanks it out.

Even though I want to approach her, I know I only have one chance to do it right, and I don't have a plan yet. So, I stay where I am, mooning over her like a teenage boy because despite her way of moving through my mother's garden like a hurricane, she's beautiful. Her blonde curls spill over her back and shoulders, and her cute nose crinkles in concentration every time she gets confused. Yeah, I'm a goner.

Felicity

I SEE Wyatt a few times in the days following our argument, but I don't talk to him, even though holding back takes every bit of willpower I possess. I remind myself that it's no good telling him I won't run, against all appearances before now. I have to *show* him.

143

So, when he appears in the window, I turn away. If I were to make eye contact with him, I'd be lost. Despite that, he's in my thoughts nearly every minute of the day. Except the ones where I'm torturing fictional people, because that'd be weird, even for me.

On Saturday morning, I'm typing furiously at my table in the rear of Java by Jackie when a throat clears above me. I hold up a finger.

"One moment." I'm nearing the end of this book, and endings are my favorite because that's when the true magic of horror kicks in. Someone survives and walks away to tell the tale. That's what horror stories are really about. Hope, in the darkest of times. That's their true magic. I finish my paragraph, then glance up to find Mayor Christine hovering above me. "Sorry about that. Didn't want to lose my train of thought."

"Of course." She looks intrigued but doesn't ask what I'm writing about. "May I sit?"

"Please, go right ahead."

She positions herself on the seat opposite me and folds her hands on the tabletop. "You did an excellent job with the festival. Thank you. From me and all of Oak Bend."

I preen. I can admit, I love the praise. Especially when I was so close to having the entire thing blow up in my face. Although honestly, Wyatt and Nadine deserve the gratitude more than I do. I might have fallen apart without them.

"You're welcome. I enjoyed it, for the most part. Made me feel like part of the town."

Her brows draw together above her nose. "You *are* part of the town. We've officially adopted you, Felicity Bell. Or haven't you seen..." She trails off. "Never mind. I actually came over here to ask if you'd consider planning next year's festival. You did so well with this one on such little notice that I'd love to see what you could do with more time and resources."

"Really?" The question catches me off guard. I mean, yeah, the festival went well, but I thought I was just carrying on a tradition as it had always been.

"Absolutely." She nods emphatically. "Will you do it? Please say yes, it'd be great to have it off my plate and in such capable hands."

Should I?

If I do, then I'm essentially agreeing to be here for another year, and while that may not seem like a big deal to most people, it is to me. What's more, breaking my word isn't something I like to do—it goes with the whole hating conflict thing—so if I agree, then I'm really tying myself down. I won't blow it off and leave Christine to pick up the pieces. Really, it boils down to one thing: am I prepared to fight for the roots I want so badly? Most of all, can I prove to Wyatt Dawson that I'm exactly the woman to put a little pep back into his life?

"Yes." Elation makes the air smell sweeter. I'd feared I might feel trapped or caged, but with that one word, the weight of all my troubles lifts from my shoulders. I grin, and happiness begins to glow in my heart. "Yes, I'll organize next year's festival. Sign me up."

"Perfect." She smiles back. "I knew you were the girl for the job." She stands and pushes her chair in. "I'll let you return to writing." She begins to turn but then pauses and adds, "By the way, I read *Gloom*."

My heart leaps into my throat, the glow spluttering.

She forms a circle with her thumb and forefinger. "Superb. You have a real talent."

"Thank you." I gape after her as she leaves, but she gives

no indication of noticing. The mayor read my book. And she *liked* it. How freaking cool is that?

My mood is so light I could dance on air as I return to writing and smash out what might be my best chapter yet. When I pack up and head home, Nadine's car is parked beside my house. My brows draw together, and I pause, wondering if she's here to see Wyatt. But she and Julia are both seated in the vehicle, and when I get out, they do too.

Huh.

"Felicity," Julia calls, hurrying toward me. "Can we talk for a moment?" She glances at Wyatt's place. "Inside."

"Uh, okay." I go to the porch unlock the door with both of them on my heels.

"You're positively radiant today," Nadine says as I let them in.

"Am I?" I glance over my shoulder as I lead the way into the lounge. "That's so nice of you to say."

"Wyatt isn't," Julia adds, winking. "He's miserable."

My heart clenches. Poor Wyatt. Even though we fought, I don't wish suffering on anyone, and I hate the thought of him in pain. I want to go to him and fix it. "Is he okay?"

Julia slumps onto my sofa and gestures for me to sit beside her.

"Can I get either of you a drink?" I ask.

"No, dear," Nadine replies. "Honestly, we're just here to ask you to bear with him. He's having a difficult time working through the way he feels about you, and it might take a while for him to come around."

Julia snorts. "What's Mom's saying is that he's got his head up his ass, but we hope he'll be removing it soon."

I smack a palm to my mouth to mask my laugh, quietly horrified, although I do love Julia's way of phrasing things.

Nadine shoots her daughter a narrow-eyed look before turning back to me. "Trust me, he's worth waiting for."

I smile, glad to have these women on my side and also pleased they have Wyatt's back. Much as he'd hate to admit it, he needs them. "I know he is," I tell them. "I just hope I will be, too."

CHAPTER 18

WYATT

I'm standing in line at the grocery store when someone taps my elbow. I turn, then glance down, meeting Marianne's cheerful gaze.

"I've just been talking to your lady-friend," she tells me, without any form of greeting.

Realizing she means Felicity, I start to correct her. "Oh, she's not—"

"It's so lovely of her to agree to organize the festival for a second time. It's a load off Christine's mind."

"Wait, what?" Felicity is planning the festival again next year? When did that happen? There's no way she'd commit to something so far in the future.

"She managed to run everything so smoothly, even with the permit issue and the over-zealous pumpkin growers," she carries on, reaching up to fluff a section of her pink hair. "I just can't wait to see what she does next year."

"You must be mistaken," I say, nodding to the cashier as I begin unloading my basket on the counter.

"No." The crinkles around her eyes deepen as she squints in thought. "No, definitely not. I saw her less than an hour ago, and she told me so herself. Quite excited about it, in fact." She smiles again. "Such a nice girl. You got lucky there."

She's staying?

Fucking hell, she's actually staying. I'm the biggest moron ever.

"That's one word for it," I reply, paying the bill. As I gather my shopping bags, Marianne's sentiment stays with me. I bid her goodbye and carry my purchases out to the car. I don't feel lucky, but I'm beginning to think I was wrong about far more things than I'd like to admit. Felicity is settling in Oak Bend, and while I'm relieved to know she's going to be around, part of me is filled with dread because the surprise I've been planning to woo her might be too little, too late.

During the drive home, an awful truth descends on me: Felicity was right. I pushed her away because I was afraid. Now, she's proved my assumptions wrong, and I don't know what to do about it. I can't leave our argument to fester for another couple of days while I get my ducks in a row. I need to act *now*.

That's why, fifteen minutes later, I find myself standing on her doorstep, metaphorical hat in hand, ready to make an ass of myself. When she opens the door, the sight of her renders me speechless. She looks good. So fucking good. How is that fair when I've heard from a reliable source that I could be mistaken for hell warmed over?

"Wyatt," she says, her perfect pink lips refusing to form the smile I ache to see. "Would you like to come in?"

Huh. I'm struck by the strange sensation she's been waiting for me. She walks inside, leaving the door open, and vanishes from view. Once I get my shit together, I hurry after her.

"Can we talk?"

"Of course." She chooses two mugs from a kitchen drawer, then spoons instant coffee into each. The jug is already heating. Was she expecting me, or is she just much better at bouncing back from surprises than I am? Perhaps it's petty and unreasonable, but I'd like it if she looked at least half as shaken as I feel. She adds sugar to one mug, then water and milk, and hands it to me. The fact she remembers how I like my coffee shouldn't make me break out in a spontaneous grin, but it does. She finishes preparing hers, then sits at the table.

"You look like you have some heavy thoughts weighing on you. Want to tell me what's going on?"

I sip my coffee, glad for the sugar kick. "I heard you're planning the festival next year."

"That's right." She doesn't smile. Just watches me steadily. "I only agreed to do it yesterday, but I guess news travels fast around here."

"I thought you'd be gone by then." Damn, so much for diplomacy. I wanted to ease into this. Not jump right in and come across as an ass. *Again.*

Felicity straightens, and her lips pinch together. Finally, a hint of emotion. "You're the one who insisted I'd be leaving, Wyatt. You're the person who thought I'd move on or run away. I never said that or did anything to give you the impression that my time in Oak Bend would be limited. That's all on you. You drew conclusions about me based on past actions."

Okay. Wow. She's not letting me off the hook easy.

"It made sense that you'd go," I counter. "You have a pattern, and when I called you on it, you ran."

"I'm sorry about that. Truth be told, I did freak out at

150

first, but patterns can be broken. Do my intentions count for nothing?"

Generally, intentions are worthless. I don't voice the thought aloud.

"I have no plans to go anywhere," she continues when I don't reply. "Contrary to your opinion, I belong here. This is my place, and I'm not leaving." She pauses to drink her coffee, and I wait because I have the sense she isn't finished yet. "I can see why you'd be skeptical. Understand it, even. But sometimes, you have to give people the benefit of the doubt."

"That's not something I'm good at," I admit.

Her lips twitch, and I see a flash of humor that gives me hope. "Can you work on it?"

"I'll try."

Felicity

I HAVE TO ADMIT, I'm proud of myself for keeping my cool and not launching into his arms. This is what I've been waiting for. So far, he's saying everything I want to hear, but I can't get ahead of myself. Letting him come to this realization on his own has been hard but, in my opinion, critical. Now, he has things to say, and I need to let him say them without cutting him off or assuming I know where the conversation is going.

I scan him from head to toe. He truly looks terrible. There are dark circles beneath his eyes, he clearly hasn't shaved, and his t-shirt is on inside out. He's also uncomfortable as hell. From the way he's wringing his hands and struggling to maintain eye contact, I know he wishes he could avoid this entire thing. But he's here, giving it a go. For me. My heart aches for him, although at the same time, I can't help feeling a little pleased that everything has weighed on him. Does that make me a bad person?

"I'm sorry," he says, locking his eyes on me. I could drown in those dark orbs. They're deep and tempting, and I'm not sure I'd ever want to come out. They also whisper secrets to me. They tell me he wants me. That he's desperate to shed my clothes, but he's resisting the urge because our relationship—and future—is more important. Somehow, seeing all of that is the sexiest thing ever, and no matter how inappropriate it is, heat begins to pool low in my belly.

"I shouldn't have jumped to conclusions and pushed you away." He rakes his fingers through his hair, leaving the ends tousled. "You were right about that, and I regret it."

I swallow and nod. It's my turn to fess up to my part in this mess. "I'm sorry too. You were right to call me out on my habit of running. I didn't want to acknowledge it because seeing the truth meant admitting that I've been self-sabotaging for years, but I've owned up to it now. In my heart, I know it's not what's best for me, and anytime I catch myself falling into old habits, I'll remind myself how rewarding it can be to stick through the tough times because the good times are so worth it."

"I'm glad you've been able to see that." He swallows. "I'm not gonna lie, I'm still scared about losing you, because it's like I've been sleeping and you've woken me up again. It sounds like you're scared too, but I hope you'll agree that love is worth the risk." He sits forward and takes my hand. "I love you, Felicity."

Oh, wow.

My heart strums an irregular rhythm. "You do?"

He nods, holding my gaze, letting me see his truth. "I was an asshole and an idiot, but I want to be your rock from now on, if you'll let me." He squeezes my hand. "I want to be the place where you put down your roots. I'll help you anchor them. Be with me?"

My instant reaction is to scream yes, but I don't. Instead, I give his question the respect and consideration it deserves.

"I don't want to spend my life playing push and pull with you," I tell him. "I'm sure you don't want that either."

"No." He holds my gaze. "Which is why I'll tell you if I start feeling insecure *before* I act like an ass because of it. All I ask is that you come to me if anything happens to overwhelm you and make you want to run."

My pulse flutters rapidly at the base of my neck. "Is it that easy?"

He places my hand over his heart. It's thudding quickly but solidly. Reliably. "Nothing worth fighting for is easy, but this heart is healing because of you, and I want to use it to love you for the rest of my days."

I smooth my palm over his chest, adoring the firmness of him. The realness. Wyatt Dawson may not be perfect, but he's doing his best—the same as me—and that's all we can ask of each other.

"I'd like that." I place his hand over my heart, reversing our positions. "Because this heart doesn't want anyone but you."

"Are you saying what I think you are?" he asks.

I purse my lips, holding back a smile. "I think we can agree that we both need to communicate our feelings to each other better in future, so here goes. I love you, and I want to be with you. If you'll have me."

He stands and swoops me into his arms. My feet leave the ground. "I will."

His rough palms cup my cheeks, and his lips touch mine. So soft. A glancing kiss. The next has more pressure, and the one after that robs me of my breath. He groans, and it rumbles up from deep within.

"You are so damn right for me. You even taste like you're mine."

"That's because I am," I whisper. "I'm yours, for as long as you want me."

"Forever." He sets me down and threads his fingers through mine. "Come with me back to my place?"

His eyes tell me that if I do, he'll give me more pleasure than I could dream of. So, of course, I go.

CHAPTER 19

WYATT

As I WAKE, my arms tighten around a soft, sweetly scented bundle of woman. My eyes remain shut, and I inhale deeply, loving the lavender fragrance that envelops me. It must be from her shampoo, although we haven't showered together yet, so I can't be certain. I need to fix that as soon as possible. Felicity and I should be showering together every day. An image pops into my mind of me washing off the grime from the day, then gently soaping her. Getting on my knees and hitching one of her legs over my shoulder so I have unimpeded access to her wet pussy.

My cock hardens, prodding the soft flesh of her backside. That perfect, round ass I want to sink my teeth into. No other man is ever going to touch it for the rest of her life. Only me. I shift my hand and cup one of her full breasts. Its weight feels amazing in my palm, and I smooth my thumb over her nipple, hoping my skin isn't too rough. She's so delicate and satiny. I'd hate to hurt her with my coarse workman's hands.

She sighs in her sleep and wriggles closer. My dick

twitches, wanting more of her. I ignore the throbbing flesh and brush aside her strands of silken hair to expose the length of her neck for my lips. A sense of rightness fills my bones. This is how it should be every morning from now on. I'm grateful—so fucking grateful—that she saw fit to give me another chance, and I'm determined she'll never regret her decision. I'm going to take care of her. To give her the support and affection she's never had, and the sense of belonging she desperately wants. She murmurs sleepily, a smile lifting the corners of her mouth.

I will make you happy, I silently promise her. *I will be here for you, and laugh with you, and make sure you have all the orgasms you'll ever need.*

Another vision takes me by surprise. A little girl, with my brown eyes and Felicity's blonde curls and cute nose. A wave of longing crashes over me, closely followed by the knowledge that we'll bring that little girl into existence, and I'll get to watch Felicity swell with our baby. I've never thought much about children before, but now that our daughter has a face, it's shocking how fiercely I want her.

Slow down, Dawson. One step at a time. Now is the moment to make sure Felicity has no doubts.

I need to show her how I feel. I may have stepped up my win-her-back plan yesterday because I was afraid to leave it too late, but I still want her to know how much I care for her, and that she truly is a part of Oak Bend. If anyone deserves a grand gesture, it's her. Perhaps I'm not the type to shout my feelings from the rooftop, but I'm going to make sure no one—least of all her—doubts that I'm ass over heels in love.

"Mm," she murmurs, nestling closer, stirring a fresh wave of lavender. "Wyatt?"

"I'm here, baby."

"Good." She rolls over to face me, and her eyes flutter open. They're hazy with sleep, but completely unguarded, so I can see her affection for me reflected perfectly. "I love you."

My heart lurches, and my knees are so weak it's fortunate we're lying down. Damn, how did I get so lucky? "I love you too."

I kiss her softly, intending to pull back, but her tongue traces the seam of my lips, and there's no way in hell I can stop myself from reacting. Hungrily, I open for her and meet her tongue with mine. I press her onto her back, and roll on top, holding myself on my forearms so I don't squish her. She's so much smaller than me.

She laughs breathlessly. "I like this side of you."

"He's here to stay," I tell her and claim her lips again. "I can't get enough of you." I'll never get enough.

I rock against her, sliding my cock through her slick folds as we kiss, and she whimpers into my mouth, her hips bucking as she strains to get the pressure she needs against her clit. Her hands clutch at my hips, then grasp my ass and slide up my back.

"It's like you're made of muscle," she pants. "How are you real?"

I'm not the one who should be answering that question. The way she eagerly rubs herself all over me and makes sexy little sounds is like a fantasy. One of my hands slides between us and settles over her center. Fuck, she's hot. I dip one of my fingers into her and find her more than ready.

"Oh, please," she gasps.

"Please, what?" I ask, wanting to hear all of her dirty desires.

She squirms, and her eyelids droop over sultry eyes. "Touch me more. Put your finger inside me."

I place my thumb over her clit and inch my middle finger into her tight channel. "Like this?"

Her moan is all the answer I need. "Yes. More."

I crook the finger, and she cries out. Liquid beads on the head of my dick, and it threatens mutiny if I don't get it into heaven soon. I stroke her, my motions growing jerkier as my own state of arousal heightens.

"Just like that?" My voice is a barely audible growl.

"I'm just... I'm nearly... Oh, *God*." I feel her channel tighten around me as she teeters on the edge of bliss, and I withdraw before she plummets over.

"No," she groans, her hips moving restlessly, her lips parting as she stares up at me. "Don't stop."

"It's okay, honey." I fist my cock once, and my eyes roll back. Then, I grab a condom and slip it on. "I've got you."

I want her to associate my cock with the best pleasure she's ever experienced. That way, she'll know I can always give her what she needs. I want her addicted to me the way I am to her. I position myself at her entrance, concentrating on her face as I begin to slide in, feeding her an inch at a time. If I could memorize her expression and replay it in my mind on a constant loop, I would. Eyes burning with lust, lips puffy, her teeth digging into the lower one. Then, as I fill her completely, they form a perfect O, and her eyes widen as if she can't believe how amazing it feels.

Pausing for a moment, I let her adjust to me. We made love over and over again last night, and she must be tender. But she doesn't want slow. She starts riding me from below, shuffling her hips back and forward. My jaw tenses, and a cheeky smile curves her lips. I kiss the smile off, thrusting long and smooth at the same time. Her head falls back, and she screams as she convulses around me. That's right, *screams*.

The sound of her letting go with utter abandon strips me of any control I had left.

I pump into her without finesse, unable to think of anything except how well she takes me and how I've never experienced anything better. But I want to see her. I stop for enough time to flip us over so she's on top. Taking my cue, she places her hands on my chest for support and rides me, sobbing my name as aftershocks race through her. Her entire face is twisted with pleasure, her eyes shining with emotion. She's gorgeous.

My balls draw up, and I grab her by the hips and fuck myself up into her. My dick is a steel rod, and heat creeps up my spine. She throws her head back, her tits bouncing with every thrust, and I explode with a shout, my fingers stuttering against her skin and sinking deep enough to leave marks. I jerk and grunt as she keeps moving, until finally she's ridden me through the other side.

Reaching up, I pull her down to lie flat against my chest and gather her close. "That was amazing." I smooth a hand over her hair, feeling our hearts hammering wildly together. "You're gonna kill me one day."

She kisses my jaw and snuggles closer. "There wouldn't be a better way to go."

At that, I let out a bark of laughter. "Too true, baby."

I never want to leave this spot. If I could capture the moment and stay in it forever, that would be a dream come true. But I have things to do, and plans to make, so I can show this beautiful woman how much she means to me.

I'll move soon. But first, I want to enjoy the now for as long as it lasts.

Felicity

"Hey, beautiful."

Something soft touches my cheek. Lips?

"It's time to wake up."

Fingers caress the side of my face.

"Come on, sweetheart."

One eye cracks open, and I squint through the morning light as Wyatt's silhouette slowly comes into focus. He's hovering above me. Dressed, unfortunately.

"What time is it?" I ask, because usually I'm up and about just as early as him, if not more so.

"A little before seven."

I open the other eye and roll onto my back. "I slept in."

"Not by much." His smile is so tender I'm amazed I haven't melted off the side of the bed. "I woke you because there's something I want to show you."

I waggle my eyebrows. "Is it in your pants?" Immediately, my cheeks burn with mortification. When I'm sleepy, I have no filter, and he's brought out the sex-mad vixen that's been hiding inside of me. Last night we came together in so many different ways it's a miracle I'm capable of thinking at all.

He chuckles but seems secretly pleased by my forwardness. "Nope. I'm afraid you'll have to put some clothes on."

"Aww." I feign disappointment and climb out of bed, taking my time as I collect my clothes from the floor and exaggerate the motion each time I bend and straighten. He groans. I glance over my shoulder and wink. "You sure you want me to put these on?"

"Yes," he growls. "Before I throw you on the bed." My

eyes widen, and he must sense my anticipation because he adds, "This is important."

"Fine." I pout. Actually pout. Before Wyatt drove me out of my mind with desire, I'd never pouted in my life.

His mouth hooks in a smile. "I think you'll like this."

"Okay." I dress quickly and tuck my arm into his, loving how he instinctively pulls me against his body as if that's where I belong. He guides me to his truck and opens the door to help me in. Even though I'm perfectly capable of doing it myself, I adore the way his hand lingers on my lower back.

"Where are we going?" I ask as he gets in and belts up.

"Surprise."

I raise a brow. "I didn't think you liked surprises."

"No." He flashes that rare and devastating grin. "But you do."

A million happy emotions zing around inside me. I love this man so much. Does he even realize how special he is?

When he pulls up outside the library, I frown. "It won't be open."

He just indicates for me to get out, lips curved in a way that suggests he knows something I don't. He comes around and takes my hand, and together we approach the entrance. He knocks, and a moment later, Shirley appears in the window and unlocks it.

She waves brightly. "Come in. I can't wait to show you."

"Show me what?" I ask as she hides a smile behind her hand. She leads us to a display that has pride of place beside the counter, within a hauntingly gothic bookshelf. I trace a finger along the wood. It looks like a shelf from my Pinterest inspiration board—one of the ones I'd love to own when I finally settle down.

"Well?" she asks.

I look closer, wondering what she's getting at. But then, I scan the jackets of the gorgeous paperbacks lining the shelves. They're all mine. This entire brilliant display is for me. Emotion clogs my throat.

She wrings her hands. "Is it too much?"

"*No*," I burst out, tears filling my eyes. "It's absolutely the most wonderful thing anyone's ever done for me." Reaching out, I run a finger down the spine of one of the books. Unbroken. It's completely new. "Thank you, Shirley. This is just..." I swallow hard. "It's perfect."

"I'm glad you think so." She steps closer and pulls me into an unexpected hug. "The book club loved having you, and we're all so proud that a famous author lives here now." She gives a little laugh. "Oak Bend has adopted you, my dear."

"You have no idea how much that means." My eyes find Wyatt, but he's already watching me, and the affection I see in his expression makes me want to launch myself into his arms.

"I appreciate you coming in early," he tells her. "But we'd best get moving. There's another stop waiting for us."

"Come back any time," she calls as I wave, and Wyatt sweeps me out the door.

Outside, I turn in his arms and tilt my head back to look at him. "You did that, didn't you?"

"Nah." He kisses the top of my nose. "I ordered the books, but Shirley had the idea. She was just a little short of funding to get them all. I sped up the process for her."

Stretching onto my toes, I kiss him. "You're a big softie, Wyatt Dawson, and I love you for it."

"I love you too, baby." Releasing me, he tugs me toward the truck. "But seriously, we have somewhere else to be."

I don't ask, because after this, I have a really good feeling, and besides, it'd be a shame to ruin the surprise. He parks on a side street near the town square and we walk together to Java by Jackie. Ella places the *Open* sign on the pavement and smiles in welcome.

"Hey, you two. Come on in." She precedes us into the coffee shop and grabs a pair of mugs from the counter, handing one to each of us. "Hot chocolate—standard for Felicity, extra sugar, extra marshmallows, and whipped cream for Wyatt."

"Mm." He sips from the mug and draws back, a line of cream along his upper lip. I giggle. It's not fair for someone to be both adorable and sexy at the same time.

"Let me escort you to your table." Ella touches my elbow and starts moving, which surprises me. Usually when I'm here, she lets me do my own thing. This time, she walks me all the way to my corner in the back, where a wooden plaque has been placed in the center of the table. It reads "Reserved for F. Bell—Resident Writer."

"Oh, my gosh." I choke up, my throat constricting with emotion. "I can't believe you did this!"

Ella smiles. "You sit here every day anyway. We're just making it official." She taps the tabletop. "This is your spot."

"Thank you." This time, I'm the one who does the hugging. Ella just stands there until I'm done. Not much of a hugger, I guess.

"Let's sit," Wyatt suggests, and we claim opposite seats at the table. Ella bustles away, and I stare into the eyes of the perfect man I'm irrevocably in love with.

"You didn't have to do all of this," I whisper to him.

A dimple pops in his cheek as he leans forward, and I slip my hand into his. "What makes you think it was me?"

I roll my eyes, because obviously he's been pulling levers behind the scenes.

"We have one more stop," he says and drinks more of his hot chocolate.

"Is it going to make me cry?" I ask, because at this stage, it's a very real possibility.

His gaze dips, then he raises it in a smile that's almost shy. *Oh, my God, I cannot take any more of this man without kissing him.* "I hope it'll make you happy."

With one finger, I wipe the cream from his lip, then I give in to the impulse. "You always make me happy."

We finish our drinks, then drive the last leg of the tour, stopping outside his mother's house. My eyebrows draw together. What now?

"Trust me," he says, his hand resting on my thigh.

I nod, and he leans over to brush his lips across my cheek before getting out. I join him, and he puts an arm around me and holds me close as we walk up the path to the house together. He knocks once, then opens the door. The most amazing smell wafts out from within. Waffles, I think. Wyatt and I exchange an appreciative smile, then he leads me inside.

"Oh, good, you're here," Nadine says as we enter the living area. She places a stack of waffles in the center of the dining table, surrounded by accompaniments. There are four place settings. Julia is already seated at one.

"What's this?" I ask, looking between them.

"Breakfast," she declares, as though it should be obvious. "With all four of us, because we're officially nominating you an honorary member of the family."

"Really?" My lip wobbles, and I raise a hand to cover it. Wyatt squeezes my waist and kisses my forehead reassuringly.

"Of course." Julia rolls her eyes. "You make my ass of a brother less of an ass. As if we're going to let you get away."

"Aww, you guys." A tear rolls down my cheek. I'm such a watering fountain today. "You're the best." I pull away from Wyatt and embrace each of the women in turn. When I return to him, I wrap my arms around his middle and gaze up. "I love you so much. Who'd have thought you have a romantic heart under all that grumpiness?"

One side of his mouth hitches up. "I just wanted you to know that you're part of something. I'm not the only one here who loves you. We all do. And if you'll have us, we'd like you to stay in Oak Bend."

The moment he finishes speaking, I kiss him with everything I have. I don't even care when Julia whistles and Nadine clears her throat. Today, I truly feel like the luckiest girl alive because not only have I found my person, but I've found my place to belong.

"Yes, please," I tell him as I draw back. "I want to wake every morning with you and fall asleep beside you every night. I want mornings at the coffee shop and afternoons in the library. I want weekends with your family, but most of all, I just want you."

He holds me tight, as though he'll never let me go. "You have me, Felicity. And I have you too."

An emotion oozes through me, sweet and warm, like honey. My big, gruff brick mason is all mine, and I intend to hold onto him for a very, very long time. Maybe forever. Nothing could pull me away from him and this family who've opened their arms to me.

Burrowing into his chest, I rest my head over his heart. "Well, you're stuck with me now."

"Wouldn't have it any other way."

THE END

Thank you for reading *A Place to Belong*. I hope you enjoyed it! If you'd like more small-town romances with heart and heat, you can sign up for my newsletter here to receive a free story: https://www.alexarivers.com

MAKE ME BY EVELYN SOLA
A WIDOW ROMANCE

Next from the Blue Collar Romance Series
Make Me by Evelyn Sola
Blue Collar Romance, *Book* #3
Releasing 17 September 2021

Laci Hogan isn't looking for love when she moves back to Oak Bend. Coming home is all about Laci gaining her independence she once lost. Besides, getting over a rocky past and losing her husband is more than enough for her to juggle while raising her two-year-old daughter but old acquaintance - Cooper Stevens can be persistent when it comes to getting what he wants.

No stranger to hard work, he's willing to do all it takes to prove to his new neighbor Laci that she doesn't have to do life alone and that with the right person, a relationship makes life better - oh so much better.

Will Cooper make her see that this could be all the happiness she never knew she was looking for?

Welcome to Oak Bend, where blue-collar hotties work

hard and love even harder, especially when it comes to landing their happily ever after.

Visit Indie Pen PR on Facebook for more information.

BLUE COLLAR ROMANCE SERIES

Escape to Oak Bend where blue-collar hotties work hard and love even harder. From broody carpenters to sexy electricians, these nine standalones are packed with small town feels, heat, and heartwarming happily ever afters.

Fall head over heels for swoon-worthy book boyfriends who aren't afraid of a little hard work for that happily ever after.

Chasing Down the Dream by Jaymee Jacobs
A Best Friend's Sibling Romance

A Place to Belong by Alexa Rivers
An Opposites Attract Romance

Make Me by Evelyn Sola
A Widow Romance Romance

Just For A Moment by Kate Carley
A Return to Hometown Romance

ALSO BY ALEXA RIVERS

Haven Bay

Then There Was You

Two of a Kind

Safe in His Arms

If Only You Knew

Little Sky Romance

Accidentally Yours

From Now Until Forever

It Was Always You

Dreaming of You

Little Sky Romance Novellas

Midnight Kisses

Second Chance Christmas

STAY CONNECTED

You can keep up with Alexa at:
Website: alexarivers.com/subscribe/
Facebook: www.facebook.com/AlexaRiversAuthor/
Instagram: www.instagram.com/alexariversauthor/
Bookbub: www.bookbub.com/profile/alexa-rivers
Goodreads: www.goodreads.com/author/show/
18995464.Alexa_Rivers

ACKNOWLEDGMENTS

I had an unusually difficult time coming up with the hero of this story—perhaps because it was a completely new project and I'm used to writing in series. Stuck even as to what to name him, I reached out to my supportive newsletter subscribers for help. The suggestions rushed in, and I was so grateful. I ended up piecing together a name from two suggestions, and once I had his name, everything else started to fall into place. Thank you from the bottom of my heart to Michelle Wolter, for giving me the name 'Wyatt', and to Judy Mezzapelle for allowing me to use the surname 'Dawson', which I know has important meaning to your family because of Awesome Dawson. You both made my job in creating Wyatt Dawson so much easier.

Thank you to Lauren, for organizing this entire multi-author series. It must have taken a crazy about of work and coordination, and it's been such an amazing experience. I appreciate everything you've done. Thank you to Amy, Kim, Meredith, Yvette, Christi, and The Indie Pen PR for helping pull the book (and the series) together as a whole package. Thank you to Sarah and Social Butterfly PR for your help with promotions. This book truly is a team effort.

Lastly, thank you to the other Blue Collar Romance authors: Lauren Helms, Claire Wilder, Jaymee Jacobs, Kate Carley, Mila Nicks, Moni Boyce, and Tracey Madison Broemmer for being such an awesome, supportive group and coming along with me for the ride on this series. XX.

ABOUT THE AUTHOR

Alexa Rivers is the author of sexy, heartwarming contemporary romances set in gorgeous New Zealand. She lives in a small town, complete with nosy neighbors, and shares a house with a neurotic dog and a husband who thinks he's hilarious. When she's not writing, Alexa enjoys traveling, baking cakes, eating said cakes, cuddling fluffy animals, drinking copious amounts of tea, and absorbing herself in fictional worlds.